JACK

AN EIDOLON BLACK OPS NOVEL: BOOK 8

MADDIE WADE

INTRODUCTION

Jack
An Eidolon Black Ops Novel: Book 8
By Maddie Wade

ACKNOWLEDGMENTS

I am so lucky to have such an amazing team around me without which I could never bring my books to life. I am so grateful to have you in my life, you are more than friends you are so essential to my life.

My wonderful beta team, Greta, and Deanna who are brutally honest and beautifully kind. If it is rubbish you tell me, it is and if you love it you are effusive. Your support means so much to me.

My editor—Linda at Black Opal Editing, who is so patient, she is so much more than an editor, she is a teacher and friend.

Thank you to my group Maddie's Minxes, your support and love for Fortis, Eidolon and all the books I write is so important to me. Special thanks to Rowena, Tracey, Faith, Rachel, Carolyn, Kellie, Maria, Greta, Deanna, Sharon and Linda L for making the group such a friendly place to be.

My Arc Team for not keeping me on edge too long while I wait for feedback.

Lastly and most importantly thank you to my readers who have embraced my books so wholeheartedly and shown a love for the stories in my head. To hear you say that you see my characters as family makes me so humble and proud. I hope you enjoy this Jack and Astrid story as much as I did.

Cover: Envy Designs
    Editing: Black Opal Editing

To Rebecca Plymon Coleman.
You are braver than you know.

PROLOGUE

Rolling over, Jack planted his bare feet on the floor of the unfamiliar bedroom and fought to stop his stomach from rolling. Dropping his head into his hands, he tried to wipe away his tiredness and the fog in his brain from the booze he'd consumed. His head was pounding like a drummer had set up practise there.

Glancing back, he saw the red hair spilt out over the pillow, the shapely curve of feminine flesh, and almost groaned. He had no memory of how he'd gotten there, but it obviously hadn't stopped him from taking this woman to bed if his naked state were anything to go by.

Grabbing his trousers from the floor, he pulled them on and swiftly donned his shirt and boots. With a last regretful glance at the bed, he moved across the room and took a second to use the bathroom. As he did, he checked the bin, relieved to find that not all his senses had left him, and at least he'd used a condom with this nameless woman.

If he were a gentleman, he'd stay and have coffee, but this hook up wasn't about that. It was a way of forgetting the shit storm his life had become. With the light of day came the knowledge that no matter how memorable it had or hadn't been, getting laid wouldn't change anything.

With fumes of alcohol hitting the cold air on every exhale, Jack got his bearings and began the walk to his own home. Passing several kids on their way to school as he did the still half-drunk walk of shame was sobering, and if the smirks were anything to go by, he looked as bad as he smelled and felt.

As the cool air woke his brain, the reason for his bender last night floated back like an evil ghost he couldn't get rid of. His life, the one he'd worked his ass off to achieve, was in shreds and all because of his baby brother. Will was the one person Jack trusted above everyone else, and he'd fucked him over so bad it had cost Jack everything he cared about.

The SAS, or Special Air Service, had been his goal since he'd joined the army. He wanted to follow his father's footsteps in the forces, but more than that, he wanted to excel, to push the boundaries and become better so his father would finally be proud of him. All Jack's life, Frederick Granger had pushed him, never giving him praise until the day he'd shown an interest in the army, and it was as if he'd finally seen him.

Guilt weighed on him because he knew Will had never had that from Frederick. The only thing Will got was criticism, and yet, he was by far the smartest of the two of them and the one with the most potential. The thought of his younger brother locked up in juvenile detention made his gut burn with pain and regret. At seventeen, Will was still a kid. A dumb kid for getting caught, but a kid, nevertheless.

It had cost Jack the job he loved, and he'd never understand why. They'd hauled him before his Commanding Officer and told him he'd been compromised and that his position was untenable, and in essence, he was fired. He'd tried to argue as his career circled the drain and was told he'd be dishonourably discharged if he didn't stop, but if he accepted their decision, he'd get a full, honourable discharge. With little choice, he'd taken the second option with the hope he could figure a way out.

Pushing through his front door, he felt the air still around him and knew he wasn't alone. Reaching behind him for the weapon he usually carried, he found nothing but air and cursed inwardly.

He'd have to deal with this the old-fashioned way. Moving slowly, he came to a stop when he stepped into his living room and found a man dressed in an impeccable three-piece suit seated on his sofa.

Glancing around, he saw nobody else but didn't discount the idea that they were out of sight. For them to have got into his home told him how highly trained the people he was dealing with were. Bracing against the wall, he made sure he had eyes on all the exits as the man stood and buttoned his jacket before facing him. "Who the fuck are you and why the hell are you in my house?"

"My name is James Fitzgerald, and I'm Her Majesty's private secretary."

Jack snorted and assessed the man who was tall and slim with thin blond hair and regal bearing about him. "Yeah, and I'm Paddington Bear."

"I assure you, Mr Granger, this is not a joke." He reached out a hand and in it was a thick cream envelope with the Royal seal on the back. "This is an invitation to meet with Her Majesty at Buckingham Palace tomorrow."

Jack took it, his confusion growing and blaming it on the volume of alcohol he'd consumed the previous night. "You're serious?"

James Fitzgerald stepped closer. "I never joke about work, Mr Granger." He stepped past Jack and to the door as a car drew up outside before turning back. "Might I suggest a shower and a change of clothes before tomorrow."

"What is this about?"

"I'm afraid I cannot say but rest assured, it will be to your benefit to attend."

With that, James Fitzgerald left, and Jack was more confused than ever, but instead of having a belly full of dread and grief, he felt a sense of something big was about to happen, like an opportunity had presented itself.

. . .

JACK ARRIVED at the Palace fifteen minutes before his appointment, still expecting someone to jump out and shout 'joke' at him. He'd done research until his eyes hurt, and he'd missed Will's computer skills despite his anger towards him. Will would've had it figured out in a heartbeat. He'd managed to ascertain that James Fitzgerald was who he said he was, which only intrigued him more.

What the hell did the Queen of England want with him? Dressed in a dark navy suit, he adjusted his tie and exited his car that had been ushered through security without so much as a pause.

James met him, and they shook hands. "Mr Granger, so glad to see you looking more put together this morning."

"You did catch me at rather a bad time, unfortunately. But then again, I guess when you forget to knock that's what happens, Mr Fitzgerald."

"Please, call me James and I apologise for the intrusion but there was no other way, I'm afraid."

James led him past the rooms open to the public and towards a drawing-room where two guards and butler stood beside a set of double doors. James knocked and waited before he went inside, indicating Jack should wait.

As he did, he took stock of his surroundings and began pondering potential security breaks and weaknesses. Jack didn't see code like Will did, but this was his arena, and he could look at any building or situation and read the threat or potential for danger, and he could see at least three now.

The door opened again, forcing Jack to concentrate on the task ahead, which he knew absolutely nothing about.

"Please follow me."

Jack straightened his spine and walked inside the private Study of Queen Lydia II.

"Mr Granger, thank you for coming."

Jack bowed low and took the offered hand, shaking it gently. "Ma'am."

"Please take a seat."

He waited until she was seated before he sat, aware James was still in the room with them.

"I'm sure you're wondering what you're doing here."

Her Majesty sat with her legs angled to the side, a cream skirt falling past her knees, a pale blue twinset, and pearls adorning her top. Her naturally blonde hair—because the Queen would never be so crass as to bleach it—was pulled back into an elegant chignon. At fifty-nine, she was still an attractive woman and held her head high and with grace.

"I'm intrigued to say the very least." Jack was careful not to give away too much until he knew what was happening. His life had taken some very odd and not so pleasant turns this last week, and he wasn't sure the blows had stopped just yet.

"Yes, I'm sure. Let me not waste any more time. My private security detail will be retiring at the end of the year, and I need a new one to fill its place."

Jack frowned, confused as to how this affected him. "I'm sorry, but surely this is a job for the Home Secretary? Don't they provide your security detail through the Met?" The Met being the short form of London's Metropolitan Police

"Not exactly. My day-to-day detail, yes they do, but I'm talking about my personal detail who are answerable to me alone."

"I was unaware such a detail existed." Jack was trying not to sound like an idiot and wasn't sure he was succeeding in his ignorance.

"And that is how it is meant to be and will stay. Since my great grandmother's reign, the Monarchy has employed their own security to assess threats to the family, both foreign and domestic. Along with that, they carry out other tasks, such as private jobs that ease the way for peace in our great commonwealth."

Jack had no clue this had been the case, but it made sense, and the first part was clear. The second, however, was a little greyer.

"Speak freely, Jack. May I call you, Jack?"

"Yes, of course, ma'am." He almost laughed. It was ridiculous that she was even asking. She was the fucking Queen for Christ's sake; she could call him whatever she wanted. "Can I get some clarity on the second part?"

He watched as the Queen glanced at James, and he stepped up.

"It is well known that the Queen does not offer a political opinion or get involved in state matters. However, sometimes there are things that need doing that cannot be sanctioned by the government or state. Her Majesty has the authority to send her team to do those jobs and eradicate threats to her people that she and her security manager deem necessary."

"And they are retiring?"

"Yes."

"Where do I fit into this? I'm sure you're aware of my recent troubles." He could hardly say the words even now, the taste too bitter on his tongue.

"We are aware of the full details of your departure from the Special Air Service, and I thank you for the work you did. To answer your question, I would like you to head up my next team and be my security manager."

"Me?"

"Yes, Jack, you. You have everything I need in a specialist, and nothing you have done has shown me differently. You will be paid well and encouraged to form a new team, as the old one is only answerable to the current manager. You will have six months to train and be shown the ropes before your contract commences."

"Why me?" Jack watched as the Queen stood, and he followed suit, holding in place while she wandered to the window to look out across the Palace gardens.

"James has been watching your career for a while, and you have a gift, Jack, for seeing things others do not, for evaluating things. As important as those things are, you also have integrity and loyalty." Her hands linked behind her back, she angled towards him. "Those things are important to me."

James looked at him with his head tipped slightly to the side. "What do you say, Jack?"

It had been a long time since he'd felt the burn of excitement in his belly. Yes, he still got that adrenaline punch on every job he did for the SAS, but this was different. He'd joined the forces to serve his country and make his father proud, and while he understood without being told that he'd have to keep this secret, he could still serve and make himself the best he could be. "Then yes, it would be my honour to take this position and serve the Crown and the people."

"Wonderful." A small smile hinted at Queen Lydia's lips, and she dipped her head to James. "James will go over all of the details with you and have you sign the reams of paperwork that goes with it. I look forward to working together, Jack."

She held out her hand, and he shook it and dipped his head in a bow as he backed from the room escorted by James. He had a feeling working for the establishment would prove to be his biggest challenge yet, and he relished the idea.

After hours of going through everything with James—who was a details man—Jack got home late, and wanting a clear head after Monday night's disaster, celebrated his new job with a cup of tea. He laughed at the thought of how very British that was and opened his laptop.

He had a lot of work to do researching people for his new team, which was as yet nameless. Opening his email, he saw one that caught his eye and frowned when he saw the title that read **Funding for New Security Team.**

Thinking it was from James, he opened it and was surprised to see it wasn't.

DEAR JACK,

I'm an investor looking to fund a Black Ops Security Team. I have fifty million pounds for the initial start-up and would like to arrange a virtual meeting for us to discuss this. I would like my identity to remain a secret, but you can check the validity of this email as I know you have your family's skills at your disposal. James Fitzgerald can also vouch that this is what it seems and not some attempt to form a team of mercenaries.

I look forward to hearing from you.

Eidolon.

Jack sat back, knowing he'd be checking out the email with both James, and if he'd see him, his brother. Although Will's current access to a laptop was minimal. If it were a genuine offer, he'd just been handed the keys to the best Black Ops Security Team in the world, and he now had a name for them. *Eidolon.*

CHAPTER ONE

"KNOCK, KNOCK."

Jack looked up at the open door of his office at Eidolon headquarters. "Hey, Alex. Is everything ready?"

Alex sat down in the chair opposite Jack and regarded him with the calm everyone knew the man for. Of all his decisions, making Alex his second had been the best. He balanced him and gave the team structure.

"Yep, all set. You leave for London first thing tomorrow and everything is in position. Decker and Liam are already in Malta, and Mitch and Blake have gone on ahead to Cyprus. Lopez will travel with you, as will Gunner, Reid, and Waggs. I'm going to head to Cyprus tonight."

Jack sat back in his chair, folding his hands over his belly. "Thank you, Alex." This tour had been worrying more than any other he'd overseen, mostly because of his father and the threat he still posed while he was out there.

"It will be okay, Jack. We have everything covered and can call in support from Fortis and Zenobi at a moment's notice."

Jack sighed and sat forward. "I know. I just hate that I can't find him."

They both knew who he was talking about. The entire team were well aware of his father's treasonous crimes. He'd offered to resign, but the Queen wouldn't hear of it, and neither would his team. So he was going to do his job and concentrate on finding his father and bringing him to justice in every spare second he got.

"We will. He can't hide forever. We both know that."

Jack nodded but changed the subject; that one made him anxious and failing was never a good feeling for anyone. "Is Autumn set up to run things from the office here with Evelyn helping her?"

Alex smiled at the sound of his wife's name. They'd married in a quiet ceremony, and she was now expecting their first child and was therefore out of commission. He knew Pax was also expecting. The team's dynamic was changing for everyone, with more of his team now married and in love than not.

Thoughts of marital bliss had never appealed to him, mainly because he was too busy. Since his father's betrayal of his entire family, he was even more opposed. Yet, seeing the couples he worked with in social settings, he wondered if he was missing out by locking himself away and avoiding commitment.

There was only one woman who'd ever tempted him, and she was so wrong for him it was laughable that the attraction between them was so strong. She was wild and unpredictable, broke the rules and protocol, and believed she shouldn't follow regulations, while he believed planning was the only key to success.

Her blue eyes mocked him even as they enticed him to bend, to break, and to take what he knew would be the hottest sex of his life. He'd teased her once, flirting with her, knowing that while she mocked his personality and found him stuffy and boring, labelling him arrogant and miserable, she was also attracted to him.

It had been his reaction to her that had him backing away from the blonde siren that drew his gaze anytime she was near. Now he had to face her and ask for help again, knowing she'd make him grovel. It wasn't something he enjoyed doing with anyone, let alone the woman he'd visualised naked more than once.

"Autumn is fine, and Will is still running things from here, so she can always ask him."

"Yes, he is."

Alex stood and headed for the door. "See you in Cyprus, boss man."

"Yep, see you there. Any problems, call me. Day or night."

"I will."

Picking up his phone once he was sure he was alone in the building, he dialled her number. She picked up on the second ring, sounding out of breath and his dick hardened at the thought of all the reasons she could be breathing so hard and liking them less and less, despite his body's response.

"Jack, what can I do for you? I'm kind of busy."

Her breathy voice was like a feather over his skin, and he swallowed, trying to get his mind back on what he wanted to ask her and failed. "What are you doing?" His voice was sharper than he intended, and he winced inwardly.

"What the hell does that have to do with you?"

He rubbed his temples where a headache was forming and tried to wrangle the conversation back under control. "Fine, whatever. I need a favour."

"Oh, sounds interesting. What kind? Does it involve guns or getting naked?"

Great, now he had the image of a naked Astrid in his head, and his dick just got harder. This woman was a menace to his equilibrium. "You know what, forget it."

"No, no, I'm sorry. I was kidding. What kind of favour is it?"

Jack blew out a steadying breath as he concentrated on the job and not the woman who drove him crazy in every way imaginable. "It seems Her Majesty was impressed with you when you acted as her personal protection a few months back and would like you to do the same on this tour."

"It's kind of late notice. Doesn't the tour start tomorrow?"

"Yes, and yes but this only just came through as a request from Fitz."

"Well, I can hardly say no to that can I? But I'll require something from you in return."

He knew this was a mistake but asked anyway. "What do you want, Astrid?"

"A favour of my choice whenever I ask it."

That sounded like a whole lot of trouble to him and not something he'd generally grant, but she had him by the short and curlies, and he knew it. "Fine but you attend the entire tour and work under me as your line manager, not Roz."

"Done."

He'd expected an argument on the last point and was surprised when she agreed so readily and realised she'd tricked him. "She already spoke to you, didn't she?"

"About thirty minutes ago."

He fought the urge to swear and was secretly impressed with Zenobi but would never admit it, even under torture. They worked together on occasion now, even though he still believed they were loose cannons and dangerous.

"We need to go over the details. Are you free?" He wanted it done at Eidolon to be sure it was secure.

"I just got out of the shower and I'm dripping wet, so give me an hour. A girl likes to have a bit of me-time if you know what I mean."

Jesus fucking Christ she was going to be the death of him. Now all he could see was her lying on her bed naked, her wet hands between her legs, and that was precisely what she'd intended.

"Sure. In fact, why don't we leave it until after four and you meet me here?"

"Sure, that gives me and BOB some more time to work the kinks out."

"Goodbye, Astrid."

He hung up, his breathing slightly out of whack as his heart raced at the images she'd forced through his brain with her audacious admissions. The fact was, she was probably working out and torturing him with visions that weren't happening. Although, as he thought of her sweaty and running on the treadmill, he realised his dick was just as happy with that image as the naked version it seemed.

Walking to the kitchen, he poured himself the last of the coffee from the pot and drank it, wincing as it burned his throat before going to the gym and working out his frustrations. He had a shit tonne to get done, including a visit to his mum before he left for eight weeks, a call to make to Zack Cunningham, and he needed to go over the plans one more time to make sure he hadn't missed anything. His biggest fear was his father finding a gap in his security and following through on his attempt to kill the Queen and overthrow the Monarchy.

After a gym session and a shower where he strictly refused to allow any thoughts of that irritating woman into his head, he made his way back to his office.

Jack spent the next four hours going over and over the plans for the first four stops on the Royal Tour of the Commonwealth before finally, his stomach reminded him it was time to eat. He was surprised to find it was already three-thirty in the afternoon, so he made his way to the kitchen. The fridge was pretty bare, thanks to most of the team being away for the next eight weeks, but there was enough for a sandwich, so he quickly made himself a turkey salad sandwich and grabbed some crisps, fruit, and a bottle of water before heading back to his office.

He was just tossing the core of the apple into the bin when the alert on his watch told him someone was at the gate. He glanced at the monitor and saw Astrid Lasson waiting for him to let her inside. It was tempting to make her wait, but the blasted woman would probably leave, and he'd have to chase her down.

He clicked the gate and continued to watch her as she walked through, making him wonder where her car was. She was tall and slim, with curves in all the right places. Her snug black jeans clung to her ass. Her biker boots and leather jacket should have made her look aggressive and unfeminine, but on her, it was the furthest thing from the truth.

She was sexy as hell with her blonde hair cascading down her back and her sexy smile that made him think of every sinful situation he could and how he could pry her secrets from her, and she had them. Her secrets were so deep it would take months, maybe even years, to find them all.

He knew some thanks to Will, but those weren't the ones he wanted. He needed to know what made her tick, and that was dangerous because he had the feeling she'd want his secrets in return, and that wasn't happening—ever.

CHAPTER TWO

ASTRID STILL COULDN'T BELIEVE she'd said those things to Jack, but every time he was around, her mouth and other parts of her body went off on their own merry tangent. Which she had no control over if their conversation that morning was anything to go by.

A blush stole over her cheeks at the memory of what she'd been doing when Jack called. Instead of doing what an average person would do when she saw his number on her phone and ignore it, she'd hit answer and had literally been caught with her pants down.

Now he was watching her walk across the open area from the gate to the entrance where he was waiting with his arms crossed, looking typically pissed off. Astrid had no idea what it was about Jack that made her act the way she did. Just that when he was around, she constantly wanted to shock him and ruffle his feathers. Equally, she didn't know why her presence, more than most, pissed him off.

"Jack, good to see you smiling as usual."

A frown marred his handsome face, and she noticed the creases of tiredness around his eyes. A wave of sympathy rushed through her, and she buried it deep, not wanting to care for this man who seemed to dislike her so much. From their brief encounter earlier that year when he'd nearly kissed her in his office, she knew he desired her. He could hardly hide that thing in his pants.

"Don't start, Astrid."

"Fine, be a grump. You got any coffee?" She barged past him, not showing any of the hurt she felt over his constant dislike of her for no reason. His cologne wafted around her, and it took everything in her not to lean in and sniff him like a freak.

Eidolon was eerily quiet, and she found she missed the constant hum of noise that usually accompanied her on her visits to this base. She knew her way around and moved towards the kitchen, feeling Jack behind her, and added an extra sway to her hips.

Jack moved around her and made them both instant coffee. It would taste like shit compared to what she was usually treated to, thanks to Alex and his love of the dark java of heavenly goodness.

Taking her cup, she felt the air go static around her as their fingers brushed and her eyes shot to him to see if he'd noticed, but he was already walking away.

"Let's go to the office and we can get this over with."

Astrid rolled her eyes. "Way to make a girl feel wanted, Jack."

He didn't answer her but kept walking until he was seated behind his desk. "Take a seat, and I'll go over the operational brief with you."

Astrid slid into the seat opposite and crossed her long legs. She was tall for a woman at five feet eight inches, but around the men she worked with on occasion she felt tiny most of the time, which was a nice change. She got her height from her dad, but everything else was her mother. Her sister was the polar opposite. She'd inherited her mom's size and her father's dark looks.

Everyone had always been shocked when they'd said they were sisters because they looked so different, but they were close, or at least they had been. Thoughts of her sister inevitably brought the familiar pain in her chest, and only iron control stopped her from reaching up and trying to rub the pain away. It didn't work anyway—it never worked.

Plastering a smile on her face, she locked the thoughts down, not wanting Jack to see that vulnerable, exposed side. He had made it clear he didn't like her, and she was damned if she'd share her pain with him. "So, what's the plan?"

He was watching her intently with those baby blue eyes that seemed to see everything and nothing at the same time. Her skin prickled with need and her heart beat faster. He was so intense and like every time before, she wondered what it would be like for a man like him to lose control, to show the world what was underneath all that muscle and good looks. She wanted that. Who wouldn't? Jack was a fine specimen of a man, if not the best she'd seen, and she'd seen more than her share of handsome men. Charm was definitely not part of his package though.

"Why are you staring? Is my boob hanging out or something?" She looked down, pretending to check when really, she was just trying to get away from the knowing eyes that seemed to be seeing through her armour today.

"Why do you do that?" His voice was a deep rich baritone that made her think of sweaty sex.

"Do what?"

"That. Deflect attention by being annoying and provocative."

Astrid gripped her coffee mug tighter, her fingers turning white on the cup. "I'm not."

"Yes, you are. You try to wind me up and get a reaction from me like a fifteen-year-old girl."

"Wow, conceited much?"

Jack stood and moved to her side of the desk, leaning his delectable ass against it. She refused to move even though she wanted to get away from his addictive pull and his leg innocently brushing hers.

"I'm not being conceited. You admitted it in Taamira's hotel room, remember?"

She did remember that and felt heat rush to her cheeks at getting caught lusting after the sexy asshole. Astrid waved her hand in the air. "That was a minor aberration and I'm over it now."

"Are you? That's a shame."

His leg pressed against her thigh, and she felt her breathing increase as she tried to stop her damned heart from exploding. "Are you flirting with me, Jack?"

He shrugged his big shoulders. "Maybe. But as you say, you're over it, so it makes no odds." Before she could react, he handed her a thick A4 envelope and moved back to the safety of his side. "We have a lot to get through, so let's get started."

He was all business again, and it was as if that little flirtation had never happened. Whether he meant it or was using it to tip the balance in his favour again, she didn't know, but she had no intention of finding out. Jack Granger was dangerous, and not just because he killed people but because he was the first person in a long time to really see through her shell to the vulnerable woman beneath.

"You'll act as you did on the previous operation as the Queen's personal lady in waiting. When she's outside of her private rooms, you'll accompany her to all engagements. Once inside, she'll be guarded by one of the Eidolon team."

"Have there been any actionable threats?" Astrid might be a flake where this man was concerned, but she was also good at her job and a professional.

"No, but as you know, there are outstanding threats that have made it clear they want her dead, and I don't just mean my father."

She knew it took a lot for him to say those words and had to give him kudos for facing it head on. "I'll be kept updated on all threats, minor or otherwise?" she asked as she read over the packed itinerary.

Jack linked his fingers together on his desk, leaning in slightly. "Yes, absolutely full transparency."

"There are a lot of formal functions and walkabouts."

He sighed. "I know, and I tried to talk her out of some, but she wouldn't hear of it. So we go with the flow."

"I'm going to have to ship some of the clothes I'll need."

"Have Pax take care of it and bill Eidolon or buy new stuff when you get to each location, and we'll arrange for it to be delivered."

"I can get Pax to handle it. She knows my size and style and will keep it appropriate for the job. What about weapons?"

"All guards will be carrying handguns and their own personal choice of weapons, but only the registered stuff will get through passport control so be aware of that. If you have specific items you can't live without, let me know, and I'll have them shipped with our stuff when we fly out."

"This looks fine so far. I'll read the rest tonight after I pack. Should I meet you and the team here tomorrow?"

"Yes, and I need you to sign a contract."

"I didn't sign one last time."

"I know, but this is a long-term assignment."

"Fine, give it here." Astrid took her time reading over the contract, which was detailed but not unreasonable and signed.

"That was quick."

Astrid raised an eyebrow. "You do know what my previous job was before Zenobi, right?"

"You're former CIA. Disavowed when your team got caught in South America."

Astrid wanted to laugh at the simplistic way he said it when it was anything but simple. "Yeah, in a nutshell."

"Maybe you can tell me about it one day?"

Was he offering the hand of friendship to her? "Surely Will has picked apart the details and relayed them to you already?"

Jack didn't even try to lie, and she found that was another point in his favour and hated to feel another chink in her armour where he was concerned. Maybe grumpy Jack was safer than honest Jack. "He has, but I'd like to hear it from you."

That was surprising and rattled her a little. "Maybe one day." Astrid wasn't sure exactly what he thought he knew, but he certainly didn't know all of it. After all, the reports documenting events were written by the people who'd betrayed her.

Feeling exposed suddenly, she stood and wiped her hands down her legs. His eyes followed her movements as he slowly stood, too. "I should get going. I have a lot to get done before the morning."

Jack walked her to the door, and she felt awkward for the first time. Her snark and attitude had somehow left her hanging. She held the envelope up to him. "I'll read this tonight, promise."

He nodded, his lips twitching slightly, and she couldn't pull her eyes away from his mouth. He had his hands in the pockets of his black trousers, and she refused to look down and see the way it pulled the fabric taut across his thighs and other areas she wouldn't think about.

"I'll see you in the morning. We leave at five am sharp, so don't be late."

"I'm never late." Her reply was terse and prim, and the lip twitch grew, making her shake her head at him. "You're impossible, you know that?"

"So I'm told."

Having no response, she walked back towards the road where her car was waiting.

"Astrid!"

She turned to see him still watching her. "What now?"

"Say hello to BOB for me later."

She'd thought she'd got away with that, but he'd proved once again that he missed nothing. Having no response, she gave him the middle finger salute and put even more strut into her stride, earning her a deep chuckle she just knew would haunt her dreams that night.

CHAPTER THREE

THEY WERE a week into the tour, and so far, everything had gone perfectly. Any other person would be thrilled by that, but Jack wasn't any other person, and the status quo made him antsy. Malta had been uneventful, and as they came to the last two days in Cyprus, the same was true of that.

He'd shed his suit jacket as soon as he'd walked in his room, the heat of the island almost blistering in its intensity and they hadn't even hit Australia yet, where it would be even hotter. A knock on the door had him looking up and moving quickly to answer it. They had a team brief in half an hour, and it was most likely Alex wanting to catch up first.

"Hey, Alex, come on in and grab a drink."

Alex had changed into shorts and a shirt and looked like a tourist, which was part of his role in order to get intel from the staff and blend in with other people.

Jack loosened his tie and drew it over his head, hating that he had to wear it, but he needed to fit in with the rest of the detail. "Any intel you need to share before we meet the others?"

Currently, Blake and Liam were on duty outside the Queen's

quarters, which was a private resort used for foreign dignitaries. It gave them space and privacy with the added bonus of acres of land and a private beach, accessible only via the property.

"Nothing that I'm hearing. The people love her. We've had a few emails which Will has worked through and he found no substance in any of them, so all is quiet."

"Okay, that makes me worried." Jack pursed his lips as he took a bottle of apple juice from the fridge and drank it.

"Only you would see quiet as a bad thing, Jack."

"Yeah, maybe but having a threat and dealing with it is better than not seeing one."

"True."

They walked to the study that was set up as the operational command room and found Lopez at his terminal working. He glanced up, acknowledged them, and went back to whatever he was doing. Decker and Mitch followed in behind them with Gunner. Waggs and Astrid entered shortly after.

Jack did everything in his power not to look at Astrid and failed. Something had changed between them in the last week. He had no idea what, just that he suddenly saw past the front she put on to the vulnerability below. Not weakness. Nobody could ever call a woman like Astrid Lasson weak. She'd survived more than most people went through in a lifetime, and he knew that wasn't even the half of it.

"Where's Reid?"

Waggs crossed his arms over his chest and leaned against the door as he spoke. "He had a call from Clay and will be here in a sec."

"Okay, let's get started."

They went over the next three days on the agenda and discussed any issues they were finding with security. "Astrid, anything from your end?"

She'd been unusually quiet the last few days, and he found he didn't like it. It was as though somebody had dimmed her spark, and he had the unreasonable desire to hurt anyone that caused her smile to fade in any way.

"Nothing to speak of. The Queen's one lady in waiting is very wary of me and a bit snarky, but I don't think she's an issue. I'll keep a close watch on her and report anything that seems off."

"Unfortunately, some people still believe that we live in four-teenth-century France and the Royal Court is the place of favour," Decker mused aloud.

Astrid snorted in a truly unladylike fashion and grinned. "Ain't that the truth."

He smiled despite himself because it reached her eyes this time.

The meeting carried on for another hour and broke up, with everyone having a few hours to themselves before Blake and Liam swapped out with Reid and Waggs. He had calls to make—one to his brother and one to put into Zack too. He did none of those things. Instead, he watched as Astrid threw a beach bag over her shoulder and walked down to the private beach. He found himself moving after her, despite knowing damn well he should leave her in peace.

Looking out over the cliff edge towards the beach below, he saw Astrid pick her way through the rocks before finding a spot she deemed suitable and laying her bag down. The slight breeze from the ocean blew her blonde hair as she stretched upwards and drew her cover-up over her head, revealing a tiny green bikini underneath.

Jack had seen his share of beautiful women and was surrounded by them daily, but none of them affected him the way Astrid did, and he didn't like it one bit. He wasn't made for marriage and babies. It wasn't that he didn't want them, it was more he wasn't prepared to open himself up and make himself a target the way that kind of love did.

He wasn't opposed to relationships and loved that his friends and brother had found love, but for him, it got in the way of order and took away his control. All his life he'd had it drummed into him by the father he now hated with a passion that control was the answer. Yet, here he was, longing for something he'd never wanted before and it fucking terrified him.

He had to focus, first and foremost, on keeping the Queen safe, and secondly, on finding the man who, despite everything he'd done, Jack wanted to save.

He watched Astrid move to the sea and walk in like she was the star of a fantasy movie before diving beneath the waves and swimming. His feet hit the sand, and he realised he'd stepped closer until he was now on the beach, the taste of salt in the air around him, the sun beating down. It was paradise at this moment, and he selfishly wanted to take it for himself.

He sat beside the towel she'd laid out with a giant pink flamingo on it and waited. For what, he wasn't sure. Sitting there waiting for her brought nothing but complications he didn't need, but he didn't move.

Several minutes later he was spellbound as she walked from the sea like a wet dream, her step stuttering when she saw him before continuing on as if he wasn't there. She picked up the towel, and he felt water droplets fall on his skin and couldn't resist looking up.

"What are you doing here, Jack?"

She sounded flat, not herself, and he again found himself wondering what had put the desolation in her voice. "I don't know." He hadn't expected to admit that truth to her, knowing it gave away more than he wanted.

Astrid sat on the sand next to him in silence, and for a while, they let the peace and quiet soothe the rough edges they were both feeling.

"I hate the sea, and yet, it has a beauty that's so raw and mysterious."

She turned to him, but he kept his eyes on the water. "How can anyone hate the sea?"

Her voice was soft, gentle like a balm on an open wound. Her accent was slight, but he could pick out the southern notes of her Georgia roots.

"When I was six years old, my father threw me in the sea and told me to swim. I was scared of the water and not a strong swimmer, so the sea terrified me. His way of making me face the fear was to watch me almost drown until I was so tired, I almost did."

"Oh my God, what a monster. Who does that to a child?"

"He believed that if I were forced to confront it, I'd overcome it. He didn't speak to me for a week after he pulled me out of the water. I was so ashamed of failing him that I vowed to never again fail at anything."

He felt the light touch of her hand on his arm. "You were a child, Jack."

He nodded silently before turning to her and seeing the sun on her skin, the anger and outrage for a child she didn't know on her face. He felt lost, adrift, as much now as he had in that sea. "I know, but we're taught to love and respect our parents and even as a grown man, I still sought his approval. I learned to swim in the sea and can swim miles now, but he took every ounce of pleasure from it. Until today."

Her fingers flexed on his skin, and he knew he should pull the words back but for the first time in a long time, he was doing what felt good rather than what was right.

"Jack."

He leaned in and cupped her face, bringing her close, his lips whispering over hers. "Tell me to stop." Half of him wanted her to put the brakes on this madness, and the other half craved the taste of her more than his next breath.

She decided for him when she sealed her lips over his, and he was lost. She tasted of the sea with a hint of sweetness he couldn't place. Her lips were soft and lush under his own as she met him at every turn. Giving and taking with the passion he'd always seen in her, even when he hadn't wanted to. It was always destined to be fireworks between them, their personalities too opposed.

He flicked the seam of her lips with his tongue, and she opened for him on a breathy sigh that went straight to his cock. He took control, tipping her head so he could feast on her mouth with nips that made her moan as she pushed her fingers into the hair at his nape, her short fingernails scoring his skin and making him want to hear his name on her lips.

It was a kiss like no other, drugging, and sensual, yet passionate and carnal. He'd had sex that felt less substantial than this, less erotic and consuming. The realisation made him pull away. Releasing her hands from his neck, he put a foot of space between them. "I'm sorry. I shouldn't have done that."

He was breathing hard, trying to control the need to wipe the look of betrayal from her face with another kiss. Astrid's hurt turned to anger in a second, the heated look going from carnal to deadly and God help him, but he wanted her just as much when she was glaring at him as he did when she had her hands on him.

"You're a jerk, Jack." She stood, throwing her towel in her backpack and dropping the cover-up over her head as he stood too.

"I'm sorry."

Her eyes shot flames at him, and he remembered the deadly woman he was messing with. "What for?"

"Kissing you." He knew it was the wrong thing to say the second he said it, and he didn't even mean it. He wanted to regret it, but the truth was, he didn't. Not at all, but it was too late to take it back now as she stormed up the beach. "Astrid."

She spun on her heel. "You know what, Jack, stay away from me. I don't need you making me feel less. I've worked hard to be the woman I am, and despite some setbacks, I think I'm pretty awesome. So if you want to play, find someone else because I'm not interested."

She walked away, and he let her, his mind still stuck on the fact that someone in her past had made her feel less, and he wanted to hunt the bastard down and kill him for ever making a woman like Astrid believe she was anything less than amazing.

Facing the sea again, he knew he'd crossed a line by kissing her, but it wasn't the one she thought he meant. His only regret was that now he'd tasted her, he knew there was no going back.

CHAPTER FOUR

ASTRID SWIPED AWAY angry tears from her cheeks as she paced her room. The tears weren't for Jack. He'd caught her at a weak moment when her defences were down. The kiss had been more than she'd hoped for. She'd known it would be amazing, but as usual, Jack had exceeded her expectations.

Jack pulling away with regret shouldn't have surprised her though. She'd never been the woman who made men stick around. Oh, she could attract them with little more than a smile but keeping them had never worked out for her. She was fine with that because she'd never wanted that either. She was too strong, too self-sufficient, and men found that intimidating.

Even her fiancé had walked away saying he found her emasculating. The worst thing about that period in her life had been the realisation that she wasn't upset or heartbroken, not as she should have been. Humiliated, yes, but she hadn't cried herself to sleep because Lorenzo had left.

That was when she'd realised she wanted what her parents had. A real, deep, passionate love she hadn't seen with anyone else. At least until she saw her friends at Zenobi fall in love and find that exact thing.

She stopped and sat on the bed, flopping back so she was lying on the cool, cotton sheets. Jack was dangerous to her because she could see herself falling for him, and it was becoming clear he didn't feel the same. He wanted her, that much was true, but he could crack her heart in two if she let him in and he walked away. It would leave her shattered.

He wouldn't do it because he was a pig. She'd seen the way he cared for his team and his friends and went out of his way to help them, but he was closed off. The moment they'd shared by the beach, and his honest admission, had sparked a hope that maybe she was wrong and he had more to offer her. His swift retreat and the regret she saw in his eyes after, had solidified her decision to stay away.

A roll in the sheets with him would probably be magnificent. She had no doubt a man like Jack knew his way around a woman's body, but she was a survivor, and her heart was more important than any orgasm he could give her.

Standing, she went to the bathroom and flipped on the shower. She needed to wash the salt from the sea out of her hair. Then she'd go and find herself a nice fruity drink with an umbrella and forget the man who dominated her secret fantasies.

As she stripped and stepped into the shower, letting the warm water rinse away the sand that was everywhere, her mind went back to the original reason she'd sought the refuge of the sea—her sister.

It had been four years since she'd last seen Adeline and she missed her terribly, but it was not knowing what happened to her that kept her awake at night. Wondering if she was alive or dead, if the agency that had disavowed her had done the same to her sister or if she genuinely was dead. Neither of them had ever planned to go into the spy game. She'd wanted to be a nurse, a teacher, and had finally settled on joining the army.

Adeline was the brains of the family and a scientific genius. She'd gone to college and straight into what Astrid had thought was a tedious job. That was until the CIA had recruited her and she'd discovered her sister was a spy.

They'd never had the chance to work together though. Her sister had been killed on an op in South China or so they said.

Towelling off her body, Astrid banished the rest of her thoughts knowing it wouldn't do any good to wonder the *what-ifs*. Slipping on a pair of cream capri pants and a pink lace top, she slid her feet into flat ballerina pumps and shoved her hair into a ponytail. A hint of mascara to brighten her eyes and some gloss on her lips, and she felt ready to face the world again and more importantly, Jack.

She should apologise to him for her over-reaction and tell him she agreed it had been a mistake and shouldn't—no—couldn't happen again. She had no intention of telling him why; her sister wasn't his to know about. Although she suspected he knew bits and pieces because of Will.

The bar area, which was more of a sunroom facing the sea and cliffs, only had Decker and Lopez in it when she arrived. She ordered a pineapple juice and half a malibu shot because she was a light-weight and didn't want to feel the effects of the alcohol when she was here. Technically, she was off duty, but she knew she was never truly off the clock on a tour like this one. If the Queen called, you answered. Day or night.

Taking her drink she turned, not sure if she should join the men or not. She was there as part of the team but was still an outsider.

"Astrid, come join us." Lopez waved her over, and she smiled, happy he'd taken that awkward moment away for her.

"What are you guys up to?"

Pulling out a chair, she sat beside Decker. The two men couldn't be more different. Decker thought dressing down meant taking off his suit jacket and leaving his vest and tie on, and Lopez seemed to live in jeans and tees. That wasn't the only difference. She'd noticed that Decker was reserved, slow to anger, and watchful, whereas Lopez was a real Latino, quick to anger, quick to cool off, friendly, and enjoyed a joke. She wondered if it was a front to hide something or maybe to protect himself.

"Not up to a lot, just enjoying the sun."

She sucked on her drink with a straw, and the liquid was sweet, fruity, and perfect. "Hmm, I doubt that. Who's covering mission control?"

"Reid for an hour while I take a break and eat."

Astrid knew the team could cover each other at a moment's notice, but each had their specialist focus, and Lopez's was systems control and data. Although he looked nothing like a pasty, skinny geek with his muscles and tanned skin.

"How are you enjoying the tour and your assignment?"

She angled her head at Decker who'd asked the question and found he was watching her with interest. Not sexual, but still, he was focused. God help the woman he set his sights on because that kind of direct intensity would be hard to resist.

"Actually, I'm enjoying it more than I thought. The Queen is actually pretty cool and has a fun sense of humour when she's not on duty. She's still the Queen obviously, but she seems to genuinely appreciate the sacrifices people are making for her, and she loves her people."

"Good. She likes you too from what Jack says."

Her damn traitorous heart leapt at his name and the fact he'd mentioned her to Decker. It took all her will power to stop from asking what else he may have said. Despite her decision to avoid Jack and forget this dangerous flirtation with him, her body and heart hadn't got on board with her head yet. "Good, I'm glad."

Picking up a peanut from the bowl in front of her, she enjoyed the cool breeze that caught and swept through, blowing the napkin to the floor. She reached to pick it up and saw familiar legs striding towards her and groaned. She wasn't ready to face him just yet.

His face was stern, a mask of control as he reached them. "We have a situation. I need you with the Queen in the safe room while we handle it. Blake and Liam have escorted her there and are waiting for you."

Astrid was on her feet immediately. "Of course." She didn't stop to ask why but took the comms he handed her and moved beside him with Deck and Lopez following. She peeled off to the right as the men of Eidolon went left.

"Astrid."

That sexy rumble moved through her body like a caress. "Yes?"

"Don't come out until you hear my voice, and mine alone."

"Okay."

He nodded and was gone as she jogged towards the Queen's quarters and the safe room that would hold her until this threat, whatever it was, was eliminated.

An armed Blake covered the door as Liam let her inside to the Queen.

She dropped a quick curtsey. "Ma'am, are you okay?"

The Queen was sitting on an armchair with a book in her hands and looked up at her over her sleek, stylish glasses. "Yes, of course. This isn't my first time in a safe room, you know. Or the first time Jack has had me swept away and into one halfway through an engagement."

She knew Jack had made it a policy that the Queen and Duke of York weren't held together during a threat. It had caused some argument from what she'd heard but once he'd explained it, the royal family had conceded he was right.

Astrid sat on a seat nearest the door, her left leg crossed over the other. "I'm sure it isn't."

"Do we know what the security threat is yet?"

Astrid shook her head. "No, not yet, but I'm sure the team will handle it swiftly."

"Yes, they will. I'm sure it is just a precaution. Mr Granger is very cautious and I'm sure if he had his way, he'd keep me locked in the Palace."

Astrid smiled, agreeing. "I think you could be correct."

"Tell me about yourself, Astrid. I know very little about you apart from that Mr Granger trusts you. You do not work for Eidolon exclusively, do you?"

Well, this was awkward. Telling the Queen you were a disavowed CIA agent who now worked for an all-female assassin's group probably wasn't the best move. "I was born in Georgia but travelled a lot due to my father's job as a sales manager. Mom and Dad retired to Florida three years ago. I joined the army at nineteen and worked as a communications specialist. Once I left, I was offered the job with an all-female security team based in France. When my boss moved to the UK, I followed."

"No siblings?"

"I had a sister, but she passed away four years ago."

The Queen dipped her head. "I'm sorry for your loss."

"Thank you." Astrid clenched her hands together, hating having to acknowledge her sister's death when she still didn't believe it, but it was the official line, and her parents believed it to be true.

"You enjoy what you do?"

Astrid smiled, and it was genuine. "I do. I get to travel and meet the most extraordinary people, and I'm good at it."

"Well, I for one am glad you do it. I certainly feel safer having you at my side and it is lovely to have another woman around."

"I'm happy to be here."

"How do you find it working with Eidolon? There is a lot of testosterone in that group."

"There sure is but I enjoy it. They're respectful and don't treat me with deference because I'm a woman or assume I won't handle a situation. I trust them to have my back in the field."

"And your boyfriend doesn't mind?"

Astrid shook her head and blushed. "Oh, I don't have a boyfriend." Her mind went to Jack, and she wondered if in another lifetime he would've been a good boyfriend.

"That surprises me. A beautiful young woman with the skills you possess would have a lot of men after her."

"Thank you for the compliment, but unfortunately, men find strong women intimidating."

"Ah, I see. Well, you don't have to tell me of the difficulties there, my dear. But let me give you a piece of unsolicited advice from someone who has a highly demanding job and a position of authority. When you meet the right man, he won't see your strength as a reflection of his masculinity. He'll stand beside you and applaud your triumphs and bask in the light you share with him. That is when you know you have a man worthy of you."

"You're right. Thank you, and I'll hold out for that man."

"Make sure you do. My daughter let the man she loved go because she felt he wasn't worthy of her position and she regrets it, but he's happier now than he's ever been. I'm glad for him but sad for my child."

"That's sad."

"It is, and I do hope what happens in the safe room stays in the safe room."

"Of course."

A knock followed, and Astrid stood putting herself between the Queen and the door. "Who is it?"

"It's Jack."

"I need to be sure. What colour bikini was I wearing on the beach?" She grinned at the chuckle from behind her.

"Green, like an emerald."

Astrid opened the door and saw Jack standing with Gunner and Blake. "Is everything secure now?"

"Yes." He turned to the Queen. "Ma'am, it seems an overeager member of the paparazzi tried to climb the fence that links the beach. He's been arrested, and we'll secure more guards to that area of the site."

"Thank you, Jack."

The Queen was standing beside Astrid now, and her posture was straight and tall and perfectly regal.

"Blake will lead you back to your rooms where he and Gunner will remain on duty throughout the night."

She curtsied as the Queen faced her. "I'll see you in the morning, Astrid."

"Yes, ma'am."

She stayed still as Blake and Gunner led the Queen away, reflecting on her candid glimpse into the life of the woman who had the most powerful job in the world yet still managed to maintain a seemingly happy marriage. Maybe there was a man out there who would appreciate her strength, but much as she wanted it to be Jack, she knew it wasn't to be.

Taking a deep breath, she faced him. "I'm sorry I overreacted."

CHAPTER FIVE

HE'D BEEN on his way to apologise to Astrid when Reid had called to say they'd had a breach near the beach. His brain had instantly summoned up the worst-case scenario and imagined his father was behind it. It ended up being a pap who just wanted a money shot of the Queen, but that didn't quell the anxiety he felt.

Until his father was caught, the possibility of an attack hung over his head like a noose. An attack could come from anywhere—he knew that and had dealt with enough threats for it not to be the problem. It was the fact his father could be the man he had to face down and take out that kept him awake at night.

Now he was facing the woman who had him thinking things he shouldn't be. Once again, instead of thinking about the threats and his father, all he could do was fight the urge to see if her lips were really as soft as he remembered.

"I'm sorry I overreacted."

He blinked, not expecting that from her. Astrid was usually stubborn and full of inappropriate comments. He was half expecting her to snarl at him and say something provocative, but he had a feeling he'd got this beautiful woman all wrong. He hadn't seen it before now, but part of her defence mechanism was her attitude. He didn't think it was all fake. She definitely had a mouth on her, one he found he liked. Especially now when she was almost timid. But she had more to her than what she let the world see.

Stepping closer, he could smell the scent of lemon balm on her skin. "No, you didn't. I never meant to kiss you, and I shouldn't have," he held up a finger and placed it over her lips to stop her speaking, "but the reasons why I regret it probably aren't what you're thinking."

He saw heat slash across the high cheek bones, felt the plump lips under his touch, and wanted to drag her into the safe room and find out if she tasted and felt as good everywhere. He settled for moving closer until her breasts brushed against his chest. Her nipples were beaded and needy, making his dick harden. "I knew you were dangerous, Astrid. That you could fell a man with a look or a word and most definitely with your body, and much as I didn't want to want you, I did. I do. My regret isn't kissing you because I don't want you in that way. It's because now I've kissed you, I want more, and I don't know how to handle that."

"Oh."

He smiled as his finger slid over her lips, her teeth grazing the pad with a nip that made him suck in a breath. He couldn't tear his eyes away from her. His attention on the job would slip if he didn't get this under control and he had no idea how to do that. For the first time in his adult life, he wanted a woman he knew he shouldn't because she split his focus. Yet, somewhere deep inside him, he craved her. It was why he verbally sparred with her so often—because he wanted her and that was all he could have.

Now he wondered if that was enough. She drew him like no other woman ever had and the more he saw of her, the more he wanted. Could he use this trip to get it out of his system, or would he fall under her spell even more?

"You're dangerous."

"So are you."

He could see the pulse in her neck fluttering wildly and was desperate to kiss her again. He leaned in until he was almost touching her and ran his nose along her neck behind her ear. Her hands came to rest on his forearms, and he wasn't sure if it was to hold on or to push him away.

"Have dinner with me tomorrow night after the Governor's reception?"

"I'm not sure that's a good idea."

He was confident it wasn't, but he wanted it anyway. "It's just dinner, Astrid, not a marriage proposal. It would be good for us to get to know each other better when we're working so closely."

She swayed back on her feet, and he placed a steadying hand at the base of her spine, supporting her. Her eyes, which he'd thought were blue, were actually more blue/green fading to almost grey near the iris. They were steady on him now, as if she was trying to understand him better. He didn't even understand himself at that moment and knew he was acting out of character but couldn't seem to stop.

"Do you have dinner with Reid or Blake?"

He smirked, knowing precisely what she was asking. "Sometimes, but this wouldn't be the same."

"Why not?"

His pinkie finger rubbed along the curve at the top of her ass, and she inhaled sharply. "Because I don't want to fuck them so bad I can't see straight."

"So, you do want to fuck them?"

"What? No, of course not."

"Just me then?"

"Yes."

"You don't seem happy about it."

"Honestly, I'm not. I don't do relationships and don't have time for distractions, but I can't stop thinking about you. Day and night. It's infuriating."

"I'm not sure. I want you. I've made no secret of that. This," she waved a finger at him from head to toe, "is a nice package and for some reason, I can't stop thinking about you either, but I don't want to get hurt, Jack."

"How about we start out as friends and see what happens? I won't promise commitment because honestly, I don't want it, but I'd like to get to know you better and see where that leads."

"Fine. Dinner as friends."

He leaned in close until his lips were a whisper away from hers. "And kissing? Is that off the table?"

She blocked him with her hand, but she was grinning. "For now. Let's see how dinner goes." Astrid stepped back. "I need to check on a few things for tomorrow. This lady in waiting job is harder than it looks."

He knew the moment was gone and they were back to work mode and liked that she could focus her mind like that. "I'm sure it is, and you're doing a great job. Queen Lydia speaks very highly of you. In fact, I'm sure she'd keep you permanently if you let her."

"That's sweet, but I don't think I'm cut out for court life. I already want to stab Otterly Montague with a blunt spoon."

"Bloodthirsty little thing, aren't you?"

"You'd be as well after a week with her."

Jack chuckled. "You're probably right."

"I should get going."

"See you at the morning briefing."

"Yes, absolutely."

He kept watching as she walked away, wondering if he'd just made a colossal mistake. He hadn't meant to ask her to dinner, but he wanted more from her, of her. Now was the worst possible timing but he'd take it slow and be her friend, and if she offered more, he'd take it. As long as it was only his body because the rest wasn't up for grabs.

As he walked to his room to call Will, he kept up that mantra in his head. It was just friendship, and sex if he was lucky. No emotions involved. Picking up the phone, he felt confident again that he could keep his head on straight with Astrid.

"Hey, bro."

"Hi, did you get the details on that pap we caught trying to get in here?"

"Hi, Will. How are you, Will? Is Aubrey okay? Why yes, Jack, we're both fine, thanks for asking."

Jack rubbed his eyes. "Don't bust my chops. I'm tired and have my hands full here."

"Fine, and in answer to your actual question, then yes, I have the details. He's a photographer working for one of the rags."

"So, no hidden agenda there? Just your run of the mill parasite."

"Exactly."

"Any news on Frederick?"

He'd started to refer to his father as Frederick to distance himself mentally. He knew one day soon he may have to take the man down, and while he knew it was right and he'd do it, he also knew it would cost him. They were essentially the Queen's private mercenaries and killing people was part of the job. It didn't matter how shitty a father he was or what he'd done though, Jack knew killing the man who'd given him life would gouge a hole inside him that he'd never come back from.

"I might have a lead in Canada, but it's tentative. I have Kanan checking it out for me."

"Kanan is in Canada?"

"He is now. He flew out this morning to check it out."

"Why didn't you tell me?"

Secrets were something that had almost wrecked his relationship with his little brother. They'd promised not to keep any more after it had come out that Will was the mystery investor behind Eidolon and owned the company. Jack was now a fifty per cent shareholder, but it had been rough going for a while.

"If I tell you about every little lead, I'd be on the phone every few minutes. I wanted to check it out and wait until we had something substantial before I told you."

"Fine but keep me in the loop on this one."

"I will."

"How's my favourite sister-in-law?"

"Fine. She's working so I'm home alone."

"Eating your body weight in red liquorice laces I bet."

"If you tell her, I'll hack all your passwords and change them."

"Fine, I won't, but can you do me a favour?"

"What?"

"Can you email me the background check we did on Astrid?"

"Sure. Why?"

"No reason, I just want to check something in her file."

"It should be in your inbox now. Is she working out okay?"

"Yes, she's perfect."

"Perfect hey? That doesn't sound like a very Jack thing to say. Is there a story there?"

"I'm hanging up now, Will. Give my love to Aubrey."

He clicked his phone off and went to his email and clicked on the link Will had sent. He wondered if there were any more clues to what Astrid was hiding from him, and he had no doubt she was hiding something. A better man would wait for her to tell him, but he wasn't a better man; he was a cautious one.

CHAPTER SIX

Astrid stayed two paces behind Queen Lydia as they moved down the line greeting guests at the Governor's reception. She had half an ear on what they were saying, and the other listening out for potential threats. She was armed as much as she could be in a formal dress—her stiletto had a blade in the heel, and the pocket of her gown gave her access to the small pistol in her thigh holster.

The most dangerous weapon in the room was Jack Granger in a tux. She'd almost swallowed her tongue when she'd seen him. He looked like he could slip into the role of James Bond at any second. He'd caught her eye from across the room and she felt every single touch of his eyes on her as they burned a trail of heat over her skin.

Astrid had studiously avoided making eye contact since then and was relieved he'd positioned himself towards the back of the room. She was seated three seats down from the Monarch and next to the Trade and Industry Minister and his wife. The food was high quality, but she hardly tasted it as she took small bites and pushed it around her plate. Luckily, there was some crazy rule that when the Queen stopped eating and laid her knife and fork down, so did everyone else, so she didn't have to fake it for long.

Waggs, Decker, and Liam were in the room, positioned at strategic points throughout. She knew the others were placed where guests couldn't see them, all overseen by Lopez, who was in a van outside with all his gear. She would've liked to be on comms, but with so many people looking at her, it was easier to just trust the men around her and turn the ear piece she wore off, so she wasn't distracted by the chatter. That wasn't an easy thing for her considering she mostly worked with women. Men and women were different in the field, and while she didn't believe one was better or worse, they were distinct in how they thought. Her delicate gold watch would allow her to tap into the feed if she needed it, so she wasn't flying solo.

The ballroom at the Governor's mansion was beautiful with high ceilings, stunning chandeliers, and art deco sconces around the room. Thankfully, someone had added air conditioning at some point, and it was cooler than some of the other rooms.

"Are you enjoying your visit, Miss...?"

The man speaking to her was the minister for trade and industry and known to have a thing for younger women, which his wife didn't seem to care about because she was sleeping with the Minister for Education. He was Greek-Cypriot and old enough to be her grandfather at sixty-eight, but that didn't stop him from dropping his hand to her thigh in a bold move which made her want to rip his dick off and feed it to him.

Unfortunately, her cover would be well and truly blown if she did that, so instead, she smiled sweetly and answered him as she tried to discreetly remove the offending hand. "Ms Simmons," she said, giving him her alias, "and yes. So far it has been pleasant."

He held steady though, probably thinking for some crazy reason she was playing hard to get. Astrid was caught. She couldn't use her usual flirtatious techniques to feed his ego before cutting him off at the knees, nor could she kick his ass as she wanted. Her role was to blend in, and a woman in her position wouldn't make a fuss. That was something she'd love to discuss with the Queen if she ever got the opportunity again—the blatant misogyny amongst the upper classes and especially the court.

Astrid closed her eyes, praying for enough patience not to break this man's thumb. A waft of air closed over her and the unmistakable scent of the man she'd know anywhere assailed her as she felt him close to her back.

Opening her eyes, she found him bending until his mouth was next to the ear of the man who was now swiftly removing his hand from her leg like it burned, and turning ever so slightly green. The next second, he moved his chair away from her as far as he could get at the dinner table's snug space and turning to the guest on the other side.

Jack gave her a look, silently asking if she was okay, and she dipped her head in thanks. He hadn't needed to rescue her, and usually she'd be annoyed he'd stepped in when she was perfectly capable, but this was Jack. For some reason, him doing it made her feel gooey on the inside.

Jack returned to his position behind her and she turned back to her meal as the next course was placed in front of her and caught the Queen watching her with a slight uptilt of her lips. Her eyes cast a glance to Jack before she nodded her approval and continued talking to the Governor as if she hadn't missed a beat. It seemed Queen Lydia was astute and missed very little, so why did she allow men like the clown next to her to get away with such things?

The rest of the reception was uneventful, and soon she and Jack were following Her Majesty back to the residence where they would spend their last night in Cyprus. She'd enjoyed seeing around the island, and in some ways, it had helped to dull the pain this week always brought her.

The Queen turned at her door as Blake swept the room and cleared it for her. "Thank you, Jack."

"My pleasure as always, ma'am."

"Make sure the Minister for Trade and Industry knows that the behaviour I witnessed tonight will not be tolerated from anyone."

Astrid blinked in surprise.

"I already have Alex and Gunner dealing with him, ma'am."

The Queen crossed her gloved hands over her bag. "Good."

"Fitz has the details for our departure tomorrow, ma'am."

"Then I'll say good night."

Astrid dropped a curtsey. "Goodnight, ma'am."

Both she and Jack waited until the Queen had closed the door before Jack held out his arm for her to proceed him. His hand was steady on her lower back, but not inappropriate in any way.

"Are you ready for dinner?"

"I am. I hardly touched my meal at the ball." She had been too busy fending off that old pervert and watching the people in the room to eat more than a few bites. "What do you have in mind?"

"Well, I thought as it's a nice night we'd take a picnic down to the beach. It's lit from the grounds above and will give us a chance to talk in peace."

She glanced down at her pale blue satin dress that fell to the floor in an A-line with only the slightest embellishment on the v-neckline. "That sounds lovely, but we aren't exactly dressed for the beach."

"You look stunning, Astrid, like a princess."

She'd heard more than her share of compliments over the years but somehow coming from Jack, who was usually snarling at her, it meant so much more.

"Okay who are you and what have you done with Jack Granger?"

His warm chuckle was the sexiest sound she'd ever heard and instantly had her smiling, and her body prickling with desire.

"I deserved that. I've been a bit of an asshole lately."

"Lately? Buddy, since we met, all you've done is glare and snarl at me and call me annoying."

They moved down the path towards the beach after Jack picked up a hamper from the kitchen and Astrid removed her shoes, not wanting to take a swan dive over the cliff in her heels.

"I know, and I apologise for that."

As they reached the beach Astrid saw a small fire had been lit and wondered who Jack had asked to do that for him. Certainly, none of his men. She watched Jack pull some slack into his pressed trousers before folding his large body to the ground. They settled on the warm sand side by side, and Astrid drew her legs up and wrapped her arms around her knees. Tipping her head back, she let the breeze blow her hair and took in the scent of the sea air mixed with the cologne Jack wore. It was becoming her favourite scent in the world.

"I thought you hated the sea." Laying her head on her knees, she angled her head towards him as he drew food from the basket and was surprised to see two fully loaded burgers with fries.

"I do, but I thought this was a way to replace a bad memory with a good one."

"I like that idea."

He handed her a wrapped burger and a napkin. "I think I might love you right now." She saw Jack go ashen at her words and grinned. "For the burger. I'm so sick of fancy food."

"Oh, right. Yeah, I bet."

Astrid took a bite and moaned at the flavours. "Oh my God, this is so good."

Jack fidgeted next to her, and she stopped, seeing him watching her with naked desire on his face. She swallowed the food and fought the urge to throw herself at him. So many times she'd found herself thinking of scenarios where she and Jack were alone and the sexual tension would get the better of them, but she'd honestly never thought it could happen.

Perhaps that was why she was scared now it was happening. It had been safe before, and now it wasn't, because he wanted her too and was willing to act on it.

"You can't moan like that if you want me to stay sane."

She licked the juice from the burger off her fingers and placed it on the wax paper someone had wrapped it in before looking at Jack. "Why not?"

"Because when you do, all I can imagine is you naked with my hands on you, my tongue tasting every part of your sinful body."

Astrid knew it would only take the slightest bit of encouragement and she could take what she wanted from him. Feel his body over her, inside her, making her come, but what would he take in return? She was scared to find out because he could leave her devasted, and she couldn't take that right now, especially not tonight. "Okay, Jack."

She turned back to her food and kept her moans to herself, the taste not quite as good as before now her belly was full of desire, and images of Jack taking her how she craved him filled her mind. "So, tell me about you, Jack. What do you like to do when you're not running Eidolon and chasing bad guys?"

CHAPTER SEVEN

Jesus he was going to die, go nuts with the need for a woman, who up until now, had driven him crazy. He must be sick or maybe he'd been working too hard because at this moment he'd give up everything he owned to taste her. The sound she made when she bit into the burger had hit him hot and hard, like a lash of hunger or more like starvation.

He'd never had trouble controlling himself, but with Astrid, it was as if seeing a different side to her had opened a portal, and now he was like an addict hanging on her every word. When that sleaze had grabbed her thigh and not let go when she tried to make him, he'd almost lost his mind.

Every fibre of him had wanted to drag the bastard outside and break every bone in his hand for daring to touch her. It was unlike him to be so possessive, especially towards a woman he'd only kissed once and on a job for the Queen no less. Even now his blood boiled at the memory and then, like a balm, the slight dip of her head in thanks had left him feeling like a King.

He'd saved people from drug lords, from killers, helped governments overthrow dictators, had killed more people than he cared to admit. Yet a smile of thanks from a woman who was more than capable of handling herself had made him feel more than he ever had before.

"You can't moan like that if you want me to stay sane."

"Why not?" She licked the juice from the burger off her fingers before looking at him, and his dick throbbed against the pants of his tux like a heartbeat.

"Because when you do all I imagine is you naked with my hands on you, my tongue tasting every part of your sinful body."

He saw her eyes flare, the pupils dilated in the firelight and knew the slightest encouragement and he'd have her under him, so he could play out all the ways he'd dreamed of making her come. He saw the second she closed off and respected her for protecting herself. He was dangerous and had nothing but the present to offer her, and she deserved more. He didn't know any more about her now than he had before he'd reread her file, but she had a depth he'd failed to see before. That was his loss because now his eyes were open, and he liked what he saw a lot, and not just the pretty package on the outside.

"Okay, Jack."

She turned back to her food, and *thank God* kept her moans to herself. He began to eat, hungry after an evening working and being alert.

"So, tell me about you, Jack. What do you like to do when you're not running Eidolon and chasing bad guys? Do you have any hobbies?"

The question brought him up short. He'd spent so many years working his ass off building Eidolon into the best it could be that he didn't really have any interests. "Will you think I'm a boring workaholic if I said I didn't have time for anything else?"

"Workaholic maybe but not boring."

"I guess I spend so much time wanting Eidolon to be the best and running the different arms of the organisation that I don't have time for much else. I work out to keep myself fit for the job, but I wouldn't call it a hobby."

"You should delegate more."

"I know but I like to be in control."

"Yeah, I noticed that." She smirked, and he grinned, wanting to kiss the smile from her face until she was as dumb with desire as he was.

"What about you? What are your hobbies?" Astrid blushed, and it made him more intrigued. "Come on, don't be shy. I told you about my hatred for the sea."

She sighed. "Fine but no laughing at me."

Jack held up his hands in supplication. "I promise."

"I like to knit. Not scarves or granny sweaters but arm knitting, where you make throws and rugs and such."

"I have no clue what that is, but it sounds cool."

She cocked her head and the firelight caught the twinkle in her eyes. "You're teasing me."

"I'm not, I genuinely don't know what it is."

Astrid scooted closer to him and pulled out her phone and the picture app. "Here, see?"

Jack tried to ignore how her breast brushed his arm, the way her scent hit his nose and focus on what she was showing him. "Yes, I see. It looks fun." His voice was gruff, and he knew she noticed it and looked up at him.

His hand cupped her face, and he lowered his head slowly, giving her time to move away if she wanted to, but she didn't. He just needed a taste to ease the ache inside him.

Jack placed his lips over hers, brushing over them as she sighed, opening her mouth for him as he swept his tongue over the sweetest mouth he'd ever tasted. Her tongue touched his lip, and everything in him urged him to take her to the blanket beneath them and savour her, but he respected her more than that, so he pulled back, his eyes locked on hers, his own need mirrored on her face.

"Show me more pictures of your hobby."

Astrid blinked as if coming out of a trance before her eyes dropped back to the phone and she swiped across it to show him a few more chunky blankets.

His hand folded over hers as it shook, and he felt the intimacy of the moment, a connection he'd never had before.

He stilled her hand on a picture of her with a woman he didn't recognise as being part of Zenobi. "Who is that?"

"My sister Adeline. She died four years ago today."

Jack's body tensed, and he felt an overwhelming desire to wrap her up and protect her from the pain he knew she must feel. If he lost Will, he had no clue what he'd do, couldn't even imagine that kind of pain. He knew Waggs lived with it and it had almost cost him his son.

"I'm sorry." His arms came around her, and he gave her the only thing he could—a shoulder to lean on.

She took it, settling against his body as if she'd been created to fit him. "Can I tell you something and know it won't go any further?"

Jack wasn't expecting that but felt privileged she'd trust him with a secret. "Yes, of course."

"I don't think she's dead."

"She was CIA, like you?"

"Yes, and she died on an op just after she started it. At first I accepted it, but after a while, things began to come to light which didn't add up. I began to investigate on my own. My handler found out and shortly after I was disavowed and left to die at the hands of a cartel we were chasing down."

He hated the thought of her at the mercy of men like that. She wasn't saying it, but he understood they would have hurt her and badly. He fought the urge to ask, knowing she'd tell him if she wanted him to know the details. "How did you get away?"

"Roz. She and Mustique were working the same case for a client who'd lost his daughter to the cartel and they helped me. I would've died without their help. I owe them everything."

"Is that why you work for Zenobi?"

"That and the fact I'm good at what I do, and it allows me to carry on looking for Adeline."

"You *are* good at what you do." Jack leaned forward, making her sit up and face him as her phone fell to the blanket. "Let me help you, Astrid."

"I can't, Jack. You have enough going on, and these people are dangerous."

He swept her hair from her cheek with his thumb. "I'm dangerous, Astrid."

"I know, but these people don't care who they kill, and I have to be careful not to expose Adeline by finding her. If she's stayed hidden this long, it's because she's scared, and I don't want to put her at risk."

"Even more reason to let me help you."

"What about your father? You have your hands full already."

Jack knew this was something he could do for her. He couldn't offer her a future but this he could do. "You let me worry about him."

Astrid looked away to the sea as if trying to make up her mind.

The alarm on his watch beeped, and he looked down at the message from Lopez.

Security breach on the beach.

"Fuck."

"What is it?" Instantly her demeanour changed, and she was on alert, something in his tone, making her aware.

"We have a security breach, and apparently it's on the beach." Jack dashed a load of sand over the fire and doused the flames as he pulled Astrid further back into the cover of the rocks. He knew it was dangerous because of the risk of burns but needed the darkness.

He quickly typed out a message to Lopez telling him to get men to the beach and turned to Astrid. "Are you armed?"

"Yes of course,"

"Good because I see three men coming out of the sea and five more moving up the beach from the left."

"Help me take this dress off."

"What?"

"I can't fight properly in this skirt, help me."

Jack helped her remove the skirt which detached from the top, leaving her in some kind of short petticoat.

"Kiss me, Jack."

He didn't ask questions just did as she asked and kissed her as the men spotted them.

"Hey."

Jack and Astrid pulled apart like lovers caught in a tryst and held their hands up as they moved to their feet and faced three of the men as the rest carried up the cliff face steps behind them.

"Here take my wallet." Jack put his hand in his pocket as if reaching for his wallet and grabbed his knife. The next second Astrid kicked sand up, and he threw the knife, embedding it in the closest man's eye.

Astrid went for the second man, and he had no choice but to take on the third as he brought his gun up. Jack kicked his leg in a high arc, knocking the weapon from the man's hands and sending it to the ground. His opponent came at him again, throwing a punch that caught Jack in the chin, but he blocked the follow-up and countered with a hip throw. The man landed on the rocks, his bones crunching. Jack followed up with a strike to the face which knocked the other man out cold.

Suppressed gunfire erupted from above, and Jack knew his team had arrived. He turned to help Astrid and saw her with her legs around the other attacker's body as she choked him out. She looked like a Goddess, and he knew from watching her fight, and after seeing her vulnerable and funny side, that he was in deep trouble. It took everything in him not to run from the realisation that this woman could be the one who changed his life forever. Instead of laying his heart on the line at this meaningful insight, he moved towards where she was rolling the unconscious man on to his front.

"Need some help?"

"Do you have zip ties?"

"The team will."

Astrid nodded, and he saw the fire in her eyes. She loved this part as much as the rest; it was why she was so good at it.

"Will you let me help you?" He didn't have to explain what he was asking and wanted to punch the air like he'd won the Premier League when she nodded.

Alex came across the sand towards him with Reid, while Gunner stood over the other men, who were either dead or unconscious at his feet.

"Is the Queen safe?"

"Locked down in the safe room."

Jack nodded, noticing Alex's eyes move to the extinguished fire and the picnic before moving over him and Astrid. His second missed nothing, and Jack had no doubt he'd be hearing about it later, but he needed to deal with the current situation first.

"Lock this beach down and have the buildings secured. Nobody sleeps until I know exactly how this happened and make sure that fire is out, so nobody gets burned."

He had dropped the ball tonight and would have to explain himself to the Queen and tell her why he'd failed. Yet as Astrid walked beside him up the cliff steps like a conquering Queen, he couldn't regret anything that had happened tonight.

CHAPTER EIGHT

ASTRID WENT to step around one of the men at the top of the cliff as Alex hauled him to his feet and her breath lodged in her throat. The air around her seemed to still as he glared at her and smiled, his bleached white teeth hideous in the beauty of the dark night.

"Puta." He lunged, trying to get to her as she stepped back, the memories of the weeks of abuse she'd suffered at his hands almost suffocating her. A solid presence at her back stopped her moving any further, and she felt a firm, yet gentle grip on her arm.

"Hello, Iago. I'd say it's nice to see you, but that would be a lie."

"Whore." He lunged again, and Alex shook him, pressing the barrel of his gun to Iago's head, tightly.

"Why are you here?"

"You know why. We want the asset, and you're going to help us find it."

"Never! I'll never help you. I would rather die."

"We can arrange that, puta, and maybe we can have some fun first, like the old days."

Bile rushed up to her throat at the images his words evoked in her mind, and she knew she had to get out of there or she was going to throw up or even worse pass out.

The sounds of flesh hitting flesh sounded behind her as she ran for her quarters, set on leaving and going where the Ravelino Cartel would never find her. Footsteps behind her made her move faster, and she got to her room, slamming the door closed. Pressing her back against it, she took a second to drag clear air into her lungs and get her breathing back under control.

She had no idea how they had found her, but she knew her position here was over. She couldn't be anywhere near the Queen when the cartel was happy to take her and anyone else who got in their way out, and that included the Queen of England.

"Astrid."

A loud knock on the door behind her made her jump and she heard the voice belonging to the man that had laughed with her on the beach and who'd fought the men sent to kidnap or kill her.

"Go away, Jack. I can't do this right now."

"No choice, gorgeous. We need to talk about what just happened, and I need to know you're okay."

God, why couldn't he go back to being snarly and grumpy? That she could deal with but this kind, thoughtful, caring Jack was impossible to resist. After tonight, seeing the man behind the front he presented to the world, she wasn't sure she wanted to either. Staying would get him and his men hurt or worse, killed. Jack had enough going on with his father.

"I'm fine."

His voice was muffled when he spoke again, "Please, sweetheart, let me in?"

If he'd shouted and berated her, she could have held back, but this sweet, caring side slayed her. She turned and opened the door, his handsome face coming into view and a wave of relief washed over his face when he saw her.

Astrid stepped back to let him in and went to sit on the bed, her arms folded across her middle in a self-protective move she knew he saw as he came to sit next to her. Astrid smiled, a thought occurring to her.

"What put that grin on your face?"

"I never thought I'd get you into my bed quite like this."

He angled his head towards her as his shoulder brushed hers, and she took comfort even that small gesture offered. "Me neither, sweetheart." He picked up her hand and linked his fingers with hers as they both stared down at them. "Why is the Ravelino Cartel after you?"

His voice was soft and deep and made her want to climb onto his lap and let him take care of her but that wasn't who she was now. Maybe once a long time ago but life, and especially her life, had taught her that she had to fight her own battles. "You remember the cartel I escaped?" She heard his indrawn breath. "It was Juan Ravelino and his brother, Iago."

"Why are they still chasing you and who or what are they after?"

Astrid should have known that he wouldn't miss that little detail. "It's a long story."

"And I want to hear it all but just tell me why this has happened now?"

Astrid stiffened and stood, moving away from him. "I didn't lead them here if that's what you're asking."

"I'm not. I just want to know if there's something you're not telling me."

Astrid paced the large room that somehow seemed small now. "You know there is, but I promise you it has nothing to do with Eidolon. It's all to do with my past."

"At the CIA? Is this to do with your sister?"

Astrid stopped pacing not sure what to do. If she told him, she risked him and his men, but if she didn't, she risked them anyway. "Is the Queen secure?" she asked stalling for time.

"She is."

Astrid nodded slowly and flexed her fingers in a nervous gesture she thought she'd lost.

Jack stood and came towards her slowly, giving her ample room to move but not enough to run from him. Reaching out, he slowly and tenderly drew her into his arms and held her tight, her head against the firm, steady beat of his heart. Astrid accepted his arms around her and tried to absorb some of his strength into herself.

Astrid wasn't weak; she was strong, but she was also tired and even if she didn't want to, she'd brought this to Jack's door. The right thing was to be honest and upfront with him. "They're after my sister. They think I can find her."

"Is that why you believe she's alive, because the cartel told you?" His lips ruffled her hair as he spoke against her head.

Not wanting to, but knowing she needed space to explain this, she pulled from his hold and immediately felt the loss of his body bolstering her bravery.

Jack pulled some slack into his tux pants legs and leaned against the dresser, folding his arms.

"When I went undercover with Ravelino, it was for intel on his drug and arms trade shipments. The longer I was there, the more I realised my handler was more interested in a previous undercover mission, but he wouldn't give me any details. Then one day Iago visited the house. I hadn't seen him before, I'd just been dealing with his brother but Iago took a shine to me."

"What did your handler say?"

"He told me to play along, give him what he wanted and to find out about his previous girlfriend. I didn't want to do it, that wasn't part of the job. I signed up as a maid, not to play the part of whore for the Ravelino brothers, but they kept pushing."

"So, you gave in and played the part."

Astrid hung her head, the shame of the job she'd done burning a hole in her chest. "Yes."

She saw Jack's jaw twitch and could almost hear the grind of his teeth from where she stood as she glanced at him.

"What led you to believe your sister is alive?"

"A picture of Adeline was in one of the rooms beside the bed. She was dressed differently, but it was her, and she was with Juan Ravelino. I started asking around. When I got the chance, I asked my handler about it, but he got angry and said I wasn't to ask questions, just get the answers he wanted."

"And those were?"

"He wanted to know the location of one of the brothels in the south of Mexico."

"Did he say why?"

"No, but when I kept asking questions, they got suspicious, and the agency burned me."

"Iago found out you were CIA?"

"Yes."

"Someone tipped him off?"

Astrid sat back on the bed, suddenly exhausted. "I think so, yes."

Jack's brows drew together in a straight, stark line; his body taut with what she recognised as his pissed off stance. "Are you going to let me help you now?"

"Yes."

He opened his arms. "Good. Now come here."

The stubborn part of her wanted to resist and tell him no man would ever tell her what to do again, but Jack was different. He wasn't ordering her around because he thought less of her as a fighter or that she was weak, he was, in his own way, trying to offer comfort. Whether that was for her or him, she didn't know.

Her arms slid around his back, and she felt the muscle against her as he wrapped her up as if she was precious.

"I'm sorry." Her voice was heavy with tears, and she wanted to kick herself for showing too much emotion, but she was tired of hiding.

He pulled back so he could see her face, his hands cupping her neck just under her earlobes, his thumbs caressing her lips. "What the hell do you have to be sorry for?"

"I ruined it all. Now you know how tainted I am."

Jack's jaw locked tight, and he looked up at the ceiling before catching her eyes again. "You're not fucking tainted. You're perfect, Astrid. You did what you had to do to survive, and that's not weak or shameful so don't take that on yourself. You're a warrior, a beautiful, sexy, warrior princess, and I'm kicking myself that I took so long to see it, but I do see it now. I see you, Astrid, and I want to help. I want us to explore whatever this is between us."

"I could have said no."

Tears tipped over her lower lids and caught on his thumbs as Jack wiped them away. "And you would've been burned sooner. We both know it and the agency most probably would've taken you out. You did what you had to, and the only blame lies with the man who touched you and the man who put you in the position where you had to allow it."

"You're a good man, Jack Granger."

"I'm not sure everyone thinks so. Roz hates my guts."

"Well, that's because you and Roz are too similar."

His eyes bugged, and he put a palm to his chest over his heart. "You wound me."

Astrid chuckled at his joke and thanked him for lightening things when she needed it. "I'm sure your ego can take it."

"Um, maybe. I have to go chat with our guests. Why don't you get some sleep, and we'll talk in the morning?"

Astrid hesitated, wanting to handle it but feeling too raw to see straight. When she faced Iago Ravelino again, she wanted to be strong and formidable, not the weak woman he'd beaten so severely that she'd spent three weeks in a coma recovering from her injuries.

"Thank you, that sounds great."

Jack lowered his head, and she went up on tiptoes, scared to see if his kiss felt different now he knew of her shame. He'd said all the right things but was he just being kind?

His lips slanted over hers, and his tongue licked at the seam for her to open for him, which she did. The taste of him was heady as he kissed her as if it was his job. She felt drugged. Her ability to function normally and make rational choices flew out of her mind when Jack kissed her, and far from it feeling less than before, it felt more, as if he'd let down his guard too.

He pulled away when they were both breathless and dropped a kiss on her eyelids. "Sweet dreams, Astrid. Dream of me."

Then he was gone, and she was locking up behind him, listening as he walked away. Far from feeling as if her life was falling apart like she thought she'd feel if they ever caught her, she felt as if something new was beginning. She just needed to live long enough to enjoy the beauty she knew was on the other side.

CHAPTER NINE

HE SLAMMED the door to the safe house as he walked in, Alex's gaze coming to his across the room where he was watching the monitors. Eidolon had a safe house set up in every town they were visiting on the tour in case anything went sideways and they needed to get the Queen to a secure location.

He'd set them up with thoughts of his father in the back of his mind, never for one second expecting Astrid and her past to be the reason he used one of them. He strode up behind Alex and bent to look at the men he'd locked up underneath the sweet three-bedroom home on a quiet street in Nicosia.

"What's going on, boss? Is this to do with your father?"

Jack shook his head, knowing he should focus on that threat, but this one was currently the most pressing. "No, this has to do with Astrid and her past."

"She share the details with you?"

"Some but not all of it. I do know these men think she can lead them to something they want and will do anything to get to it, and that they hurt her."

It was taking every single ounce of restraint he had to hold his shit together. What she'd told him about her past had affected him more than he'd ever let on to her. He wasn't disgusted as she'd thought but the rage was something he'd only ever felt one time before, and that was when he'd learned what Frederick had done to Will.

His muscles strained with the need to hurt and fight something. He wanted to kill Iago for what he'd done to the woman he'd fought not to care about and lost the battle against. No, not lost, he'd crossed that bridge willingly in the last twenty-four hours. Astrid had shown him the person under the façade, and while he was attracted to the front and the sass she showed the world, it was what was underneath that really drew him.

"Astrid was undercover with the cartel when her cover was blown. She believes it was her handler who ratted her out and that the CIA was really looking for her sister, even though they'd told her she was dead."

"Is her sister CIA?"

"Yes, she was allegedly killed on an undercover mission just after Astrid was recruited. Astrid believed she was dead until they sent her under with Ravelino and she saw a picture of Juan with Adeline. That was when she got burned and by all that she isn't telling me, almost died. Roz saved her."

"Jesus."

Jack nodded, knowing that if anyone knew how he felt it was Alex. If anything, Alex probably knew more about how he felt than he did. This was new for him and not exactly welcome timing-wise but he couldn't and wouldn't turn back the clock.

"Wanna go crack some skulls?"

Jack looked down at Alex, who was watching him with barely veiled anger himself. He hated the idea of any woman getting hurt and still had issues with Bás because of what he'd done to Evelyn. Jack now understood it more than ever.

"Yeah, let's do that." And maybe he'd get some information out of them too. Reid was seated outside the door to the secure room where the men were being held, or at least the four who had lived were, his booted feet up on chair opposite.

"Boss man."

"Jack wants to play with his victims."

A wide grin spread over Reid's face. "Awesome."

Reid keyed in the code, the door released, and he stood back allowing Jack to go first. The room was dark, with only minimal lighting and the men were hung by their arms from the ceilings with only the tips of their toes touching the ground. Hence, it gave the illusion of control when actually, by trying to keep their feet on a solid foundation, they were tiring their muscles more. The cellar ran the expanse of the property's ground floor, and as was protocol for Eidolon, the men were kept as far away as possible from each other and gagged so they couldn't communicate.

Jack glanced at three of the men before his eyes landed on Iago, who was glaring at him with hatred and arrogance in every pore. Jack sauntered towards Iago, wanting nothing more than to put his fist in the asshole's face and knock his ridiculous teeth down his throat. Any other mission he'd curb that desire and try to lead his men, but this was personal. "Cut him down."

Reid stepped up, taking out his tactical knife and cut Iago loose. The man grabbed his arms close to his body as the stress position being loosened let the blood flow back to his arms, the pain awful.

Jack bent down and ripped the tape from the man's mouth. "We need a little chat, Iago."

"What we need is for that puta to choke on my cock."

His words followed by an arrogant smirk made Jack see red, his legendary control failing him in the face of this disgusting human being's insults towards Astrid. "Shame, I liked this suit."

Jack lunged forward. He wanted this man to feel pain, and he wanted him as far away from Astrid as he could get him—preferably via an unmarked grave. Grabbing the front of Iago's dark shirt, he hauled him up and let go with a right hook that spilt blood from his nose, the crack satisfying.

"You broke my nose, motherfucker, and now you'll pay for that insult."

Jack almost laughed at the indignation the man showed, along with the fact he didn't seem to realise he was in the presence of men who had killed for far less than the crimes he'd perpetrated against Astrid, and so many other nameless women no doubt.

"Cut his feet loose, let's make this interesting."

Reid bent and cut the ties that kept Iago's feet together, and the man scrambled to stand, putting space between them. The next second Iago did what Jack had expected and lunged for him. He let him get in a couple of hits, feeding off the pain, welcoming it even as he thumbed the blood from his lip and smiled.

Then he took Iago to the ground, kneeling on his arms as he used his body weight to pin the man down. His next punch was to the man's jaw, and he heard the bone crunch as he wailed in pain.

"You're gonna break my jaw."

Reid stepped in and looked over Jack's shoulder. "Nah, he's gonna break both."

Iago screamed and tried to get free, bucking his hips to knock Jack off, but he'd spent years in hand-to-hand combat, and nobody beat him. He made it his mission to lead by example and made sure he never expected anything from his men that he couldn't do himself. It was why he spent extra time training with Sensei Dave on new techniques and perfecting the old so they were as natural as breathing now.

Jack kept going until the screaming stopped, and Iago had passed out. He sat back, his shirt soaked with blood and his knuckles raw from the power of the punches he'd rained down on the weak human being who only preyed on women, it seemed. Iago hadn't even put up much of a fight, but Jack felt better knowing he'd wake up in agony.

He turned to Alex and Reid, who were leaning against the wall watching him. "You had enough?"

Jack stood. "For now." He peered at the man at his feet. "Hang him back up."

Jack walked away as Alex tipped his head at Reid. Jack headed upstairs, where there were two bedrooms with spare clothes and weapons. He tossed the ruined shirt and tux trousers in the bin and dressed in full tactical black, which was all that was available. He should shower, but he needed to get back, and he had two calls to make that couldn't wait.

He sat at the desk and made the first call, smiling when the man picked up on the first ring.

"Wondered how long it would take before you called in the cavalry."

Jack shook his head with a smile. "Cavalry my ass, Zack."

"What do you need, Jack?"

"I have a situation." He explained the basics of it, wanting Astrid to be able to share her story if she wanted.

"Shit, that just made things tricky with the tour."

"Tell me about it. So, can you send me some backup?"

"Jack, Eidolon paid Fortis to be on retainer for the next eight weeks. We have nothing but time. I can have Jace and Zin there by morning, and the rest of us can meet you in Canada."

Jack felt a wave of relief wash over him knowing he had back up he could trust, and there was nobody better than Fortis. "Thank you. Any news from Kanan on Frederick?"

"No, but he's checking in with us regularly and thinks he has a lead. As soon as we have something more than smoke, we'll let you know."

Jack trusted Zack to do that and Kanan was an excellent spy, one of the best MI6 had ever had in fact.

"What about Will? You want him on this too?"

Jack gave it some thought, and while he did want his help, he didn't need him there in person as his work was remote and Lopez could handle the stuff they needed on site. He also wanted someone watching his mother. There was a good chance his father would use his absence to try and reach out to his wife, and Jack wouldn't allow his mother to be hurt any more than she already had been. "Yes, but he can stay there. I want someone to watch Mum, and he and Aubrey can do that."

"Good idea. I'll ask Lucy to help out with that. Maybe see if the oldies can get her to come and visit the estate and help out."

"Yeah, that's a good idea, she'll like that. I'll let her know."

"See you in Canada, Jack."

"Yeah, see you soon."

His next call was to Roz who was almost halfway out the door to come to Astrid's aide until he calmed her down. "Roz, wait. She told me what happened and about her sister. I won't let anyone hurt her, I promise."

"Don't make promises you can't keep, Jack. Those motherfuckers almost killed her before. She was in a coma for three weeks and had months in rehab after what they did, and those are the scars we can see."

"I know and believe me, they'll all pay for what they did to her." He heard the pause on the line and wondered if Roz had hung up on him. "Roz?"

"Are you sleeping with her?"

"No." He had no intention of answering to Roz about his actions or plans.

"But you want to?"

"Astrid and I, and what we do, are none of your business, Roz."

"Wrong answer, asshole. I'll have one of my girls on a flight tonight to provide my employee and friend back up. If I find out you've stuck your dick where it shouldn't be, I'll snap it off and feed it to you."

The line went dead, and while he felt the slightest irritation, he was thankful that Roz cared enough about Astrid to want to warn him off.

CHAPTER TEN

ASTRID HAD THOUGHT she knew what Jack did, but as the tour moved from Cyprus to Canada she realised that she'd had no idea what went into this kind of thing. She'd hardly seen him since the attack on the beach the night before and her chest tightened slightly at the loss. Oh, from afar she'd seen him talking to his men, to the Queen's private secretary Fitz, and even the Queen herself but as the day wore on, he looked more and more tired.

Even as she moved about the cabin during the flight Jack was in constant motion. A couple of hours before they landed he sat in the seat beside her looking exhausted. She realised despite being dead on his feet, with shadows under his eyes and the slight stubble of beard on his chin, he was still handsome.

He lifted her hand in his, and she glanced around to see if anyone was looking. She wasn't ashamed of what was happening with her and Jack. It was more the fact she didn't even know what was going on. Their chemistry was off the charts, and the more she got to know him, the more she realised he wasn't the uptight asshole he'd tried to portray himself as being. He was sweet and thoughtful and sensitive, which were all words she never thought she'd say in relation to this man.

His thumb rubbed over the pulse in her wrist as his eyes moved over her face. "Are you okay? I haven't had time to check in with you and make sure you're all right after last night."

Astrid tilted her head towards him. "I'm a big girl, Jack. You don't need to babysit me." She swept her free hand around the cabin of the luxury plane, indicating everything. "God knows you have enough to do already."

Jack bent his head closer, and she found herself pinned in place by his intense gaze. "I'm not trying to babysit you, firefly. I want to know that you're okay because it eases the knot inside my chest every time I think about you at the hands of that monster."

Astrid felt her heart beat faster at his admission that he was worried about her and wanted to ease the pain she could see on his face. Cradling his cheek with her free hand, she wanted to feel that stubble between her thighs and the imagery made her clench them together. "I'm fine, Jack. It's taken a long time to get here, but I'm okay now. I'm just angry they found me."

He turned his face into her palm; his lips brushing against her skin, his eyes closing. He had long, dark lashes and a strong manly brow which was usually pulled into a frown, but now it was relaxed. "We'll find out how they found you and help you handle it, firefly."

He pressed his lips to her palm, and she leaned in close, feeling the quietness of the cabin surrounding them as everyone else slept, getting rest while they could. "Why firefly?"

His eyes popped open, and he pulled away, a sexy smirk on his handsome face as he leaned back in his seat, keeping his other hand in hers still. "Because you're beautiful like one and throw light and life wherever you go."

"That is the sweetest thing I've ever heard."

"Yeah? Well don't tell anyone. I have a reputation to think of."

"Should have thought of that before, Jackie boy."

His eyes that had been closing popped open at the nickname she'd used. "Jackie boy? *Boy*? Do I look like a boy to you?"

His look of indignation was adorable, and while she may have found it scary before, now she found it cute because she knew there was no heat or anger directed her way. "Well, until I see different..." She shrugged her shoulders and grinned at him.

Jack shook his head and closed his eyes. "Pain in my ass."

Moments later, he was out, and she could see his breathing even out as his body succumbed to the need for sleep.

The arrival process was no less stressful than the departure, and although it proceeded like a well-oiled machine, Astrid could feel the team's tension. Ensuring the Queen and Duke had excellent security in place yet making it feel relaxed was a massive undertaking. Especially with at least two known threats to the team.

If she thought it wouldn't piss him off, she'd suggest leaving so she could handle her business. But Jack would take that as a slight and the truth was, she didn't want to go. She wanted to stay, as much to watch his back as to be with him over the next seven weeks. Plus, she'd grown fond of the Queen and wanted to make sure she was protected from any loons who would do her harm.

Gunner and Waggs had gone ahead to make sure the Queen's suite was clear and the hotel was ready. Astrid had been to Toronto before and loved it but had never stayed at the Bainbridge Royal Hotel before. It was the Queen's hotel of choice every time she travelled to Toronto, as it had been for her parents and her and grandmother before her.

She knew the hotel's logistics put extra strain on the team to ensure her safety, as there were more outsides factors in play—like other guests and more hotel staff.

The cars rolled up and having changed on the plane, Astrid was now playing her role of Miss Caroline Simmons, lady in waiting.

Delight lit her face when they walked through the doors of the hotel and she saw Bebe, her friend and fellow Zenobi colleague, in the foyer standing well back from the circus that was their arrival.

She also saw Zack Cunningham and Daniel Thompson from Fortis. She'd known they'd be joining them as Zin and Jace had arrived yesterday in Cyprus to give them extra cover and would provide help for the rest of the tour.

Astrid felt eyes on her and saw Jack in her peripheral vision watching her, the warmth of his gaze seeping through the fabric of her dress like a caress.

Once the hotel manager had fawned over the royal guests, he led them to an elevator that would be strictly for their use only and showed them to the rooms they'd be using on the top floor. This floor at least was secure as it was only accessed by those cleared by Eidolon. They, along with the Fortis guys, would be on guard at all the exits.

With Queen Lydia in her own room taking afternoon tea and resting before her reception that night, Astrid let Decker show her to her room to keep up appearances for anyone that might be watching.

"Thank you, Deck."

"My pleasure. Jack will be having a meeting with the entire team in two hours to go over the plan for the next few days and how Fortis will fit into that."

"Which room?"

"He said to tell you he'll come and get you."

Astrid saw the question in Decker's eyes that he left unsaid and didn't give in to the pressure to offer up any information. She knew the team were close like the women of Zenobi were, and they'd have questions about what had happened, and she'd answer those at the meeting. She owed them that for bringing this to their door but what was going on with her and Jack was nobody else's business but theirs. "Okay, I'll be ready."

Astrid closed the door and nearly jumped out of her skin at the voice behind her.

"Nice dress, Ace."

Astrid spun laughing and threw herself at her friend. "Bebe, I'm so glad to see you."

Bebe hugged her back. "Heard you needed some back up so here I am."

Astrid tugged her towards the chairs in the huge suite, which also had terrific views over Toronto. "Did you hear about Ravelino?"

"Yes, Jack called Roz after you did. He was losing his mind over it, wanted to know exactly what happened."

Astrid pulled her lip between her teeth. "He was on the beach with me when they attacked. It would've been different if I'd been alone. I couldn't have fought them all, and if they'd gotten to the building I hate to think what might have happened."

"Thank God he was." Bebe wiggled her eyebrows. "Talking of that, why was he on the beach with you alone at night?"

"We were on a date." Astrid waited for the inevitable warnings to come her way.

"Wow. How did you manage that?"

Astrid threw up her hands and let them fall to her lap. "No clue. We went from me messing with him and him growling at me, to somehow him asking me on a date."

Bebe gave her a look and stood, walking to the bar. "I'm gonna need a drink for this." She held up the bottle of wine in question, and Astrid lifted her hand, pinching her fingers an inch apart. "A small glass, I'm on the clock."

Bebe poured and brought the drinks back to her. "So, start from the beginning and don't leave anything out."

Astrid did, telling her about the meeting at Eidolon, the way he'd opened up on the beach, and that they had kissed and how she'd suddenly felt afraid and pulled back. Then about Jack asking her on a date to get to know him, which ended in gunfire and an entirely new headache in the form of Iago Ravelino.

"Wow, he's romancing you."

Astrid snorted. "I don't think it's that, more like he wants in my pants and I'm a challenge."

"Has he treated you like one? 'Cos if he has, I can kick his ass for you."

Astrid shook her head. "No, he's been nothing but honest and respectful."

"So why the change of heart?"

"Honestly, when I thought he had no interest in me, it was safe to flirt, but now it's serious."

Bebe threw her head back as she laughed, spilling her wine down her leg. "Oh shit." She swiped at the mark and sucked her thumb.

"What's so funny?"

"That you think he wasn't interested in you. That man has been eye-fucking you for months."

Astrid sat up straighter, hating that she was so eager to hear this. "No, he hasn't."

"Yup. He tried to fight it, and clever man that he is, he's accepted his fate."

"Up until now Jack has done nothing but snap his teeth at me."

"Well duh. That's because he's been fighting his attraction to you. You rattle him, Astrid, and a man like Jack doesn't like to feel rattled. He likes to control the narrative at all times."

"Hmm, interesting." The thought that Jack had wanted her for so long and fought it was a bit of a double-edged sword. She liked that he wanted her, but why would he fight it so hard and why give in now? "Either way, he's made it clear he only wants casual and that he has no room for a relationship."

"And do you want that?"

"It's not that I want a relationship with the promise of marriage and two-point four kids, but I can't shake the feeling that he could hurt me."

"Hurt you how?"

"Jack is so intense when he's doing something. With me, he's so focused on me that he could easily make me forget it wasn't real and I'd fall for him."

"Sounds like you know all the pitfalls so you can avoid them. Can you imagine that kind of intensity and focus between the sheets? Jack doesn't strike me as a man who has trouble finding a woman's clitoris."

"Yeah, if he fucks like he kisses, it would be phenomenal."

Bebe knocked her knee with her hand. "See, so maybe have some fun. Life is short. We know that better than most so enjoy what he's offering and keep your heart out of it. You can be safe in the knowledge that if he hurts you, Zenobi will cut his bollocks off and put them in a jar."

Astrid shook her head, laughing. "Not a visual I want, thanks. But maybe you're right. I should just see what happens and stop overthinking it."

"Good girl. Now that's sorted, let's talk about Ravelino. Do we know how he found you and why?"

"That would be a no to both. Jack had him removed before I could find out."

"Well, let me start looking into that while you do your thing. I know Eidolon is helping you. Do you want me to run this alone or work with them?"

"What does Roz want?"

"She wants whatever you want. If you trust Jack and his boys, we'll work with them on this. If you don't, we'll work it quiet."

"Work with them. It makes sense to share information. I need to know how they found me, and if I fucked up when I was searching back channels for Adeline and exposed myself in some way."

"Okay, I'll speak with Waggs and Mitch and find out what they know. Do we know where they took the men they captured?"

"No, just that it was off-site."

"I need that info too in case I want to interrogate them."

"I'm sorry you've been dragged into this, Bebe."

"Hey, none of that. We're family, and when one of us gets attacked, we all stand and fight."

"Thank you."

Astrid leaned her head against Bebe's shoulder. She still missed Adeline every single day, but these women who had saved her were like sisters to her now too. She'd do anything for them, and they were proving they felt the same way towards her.

An hour later, a knock on her door had her smiling as she swung it open for Jack. He'd changed into grey suit trousers and a white shirt which was open at the collar and a jacket she knew hid his sidearm. Some of the fatigue she'd seen on the plane seemed to have lifted, and she wasn't sure if it was the few hours' sleep he'd had, or knowing he had more support on the ground with Fortis there now.

"Ready to go?"

"Yeah, let me just let Bebe know I'm going." Her friend was in the next room with an adjoining door between them. She'd said it was already booked when she'd arrived and Astrid guessed that was Jack's doing, wanting to make sure she was protected.

He followed her into the suite and looked around at the mess she'd already made. Clothes, shoes, and make-up were scatted across the room making it look like a whirlwind had been through. She wasn't a naturally tidy person, life was too short but she saw Jack's wide eyes and knew it would be driving him crazy.

She knocked on the door, it opened seconds later, and Bebe stepped through into her room. "Hey."

"Bebe, I'm off now, so I'll see you later."

Astrid turned to find Jack picking up clothes and placing them over the arm of the chair and pairing the shoes and lining them up. She folded her arms over her chest. "You got a new job as a maid, Jack?"

She saw him smirk as he looked up and came towards her with a glint in his eye that promised retribution for her smart-ass comment. "How can you think in this chaos?"

"Chaos is my middle name."

He stepped close and took her chin in his hand, the grip firm but gentle as he eyed her lips like a starving man. The shock of desire burned through her, and she fought to keep her knees locked in place.

"Firefly, you're definitely chaos, and it turns out I like it more than I thought."

His thumb pulled at her bottom lip, and her breath hitched. Jesus Christ, he was flaying her skin with the heat in his blue eyes.

He let go and walked to the door. "Come on. I don't want to be late for my own meeting."

Astrid cast a last glance at Bebe who was fanning herself and followed him out of the room. That was the kind of move that made her lose all sense and become a ball of sexual need.

CHAPTER ELEVEN

JACK STRODE towards the conference room on the floor that was set up for the meeting. It was only two doors away from the Royal Suite, so he left two men outside the door. He'd served with some of the Fortis guys and had worked closely with the rest since and knew Jace could handle anything. Dane was equally trustworthy and competent. He wouldn't have called them otherwise, and God, did he need them. Keeping this tour going and the Queen and the Prince Consort safe was a task on its own but add in his father, and now Ravelino, and it had become a nightmare.

He'd hardly had a second to himself since the attack except for the two hours' sleep he'd managed to catch on the plane. He'd rather have talked to Astrid, but his body had recognised it was past exhaustion even if he hadn't and shut down.

Waking, he'd found her still next to him, her hand where he'd left it in his, reading a book about knitting techniques. She was such a paradox, and the more he got to know her, the more he wanted from her. She was sweet and funny, sensitive, but still full of fire and attitude. She never let him get away with his shit and didn't think twice about calling him on it.

It was one of the things that had made him notice her. Not that any of the women in his world were scared of him and rightly so. He'd never harm a hair on their heads and would die to protect any one of them—even Roz. Although he had no intention of ever letting her know that.

He walked in and noticed his team were already in situ spread out across the back of the room. The men from Fortis were seated closer to the front.

Zack approached and shook his hand. "Thanks for coming, Zack."

"No problem. We were just spinning our wheels anyway, and God knows you've helped us enough in the past."

"Well, it's good to have you here because this shit storm just became a fucking tornado."

He saw Astrid take a seat beside Lopez and had the urge to move her closer to him and away from his friend. His firefly had no idea the effect she had on men. Lopez was unknowingly walking a very fine line as he laughed at something she said and leaned in closer as she smiled back. A surge of jealousy hit him, and he wanted to rip Lopez away. He wanted to own her smiles, be the one she graced with her laugh. It was fucking ridiculous and something he'd never experienced before, and he didn't fucking like it.

Zack followed his sightline and his eyebrows rose. "Oh, it's like that, is it?"

"No, I just need his head focused on work."

Zack chuckled and clapped him on the shoulder. "Seriously, Jack, you watched it happen to all of us and half your team. Accept your fate now, and it will be much easier."

"It's not the same."

Zack shrugged. "Fine, have it your way."

He walked away to sit with his team, and Jack pressed the button on his laptop to link with Will. His face filled the screen behind him as he clapped his hands to get everyone's attention.

"Okay we have a lot to get through so let's get started. Firstly, thank you to Zack and his team for joining us. Hopefully, we can get through this tour without anyone getting hurt or having any more major incidents with your help. I'm going to run through the plan for the next few days, and once that's done we'll move on to other matters."

He caught Astrid watching him, her focus clear and on the job. He wondered how she managed to compartmentalise when his focus was shot to shit every time she was in the same room as him. It was as if, suddenly, she was the only thing that mattered. Not his job or the Queen or even his vendetta against Frederick; just her safety and him getting to see the smile she wore when she was truly happy.

Her lips twitched and she winked at him, forcing him to lose his train of thought as he looked away, needing to get his head on straight. They had a few kisses between them that would hopefully become some hot sex, and he'd get her out of his system and back in the friend zone where it was safe.

"As I was saying, Fortis will mainly cover the night duty so that my team can be on during the walkabouts and events Her Majesty has planned. There will be some overlap in that some of the Fortis crew will attend a few evening events for extra cover. It will also allow the teams to give a proper security handover.

"We have four events planned here before we move to Montreal. A reception tonight at the Prime Minister's home, which is small, tomorrow is the opening of a hospital wing for patients with dementia. The day after will be a walkabout at the new government building followed by the theatre in the evening."

"Seems straight forward." Zack crossed his arms over his chest and balanced his ankle on his opposite knee. "What about the threats we know about?"

Jack caught Astrid's eye, not wanting to betray her confidence in any way, and she nodded, giving him permission. "As you know, we have the threat from Frederick Granger still hanging over us, and we've had a sighting here in Canada. Which was confirmed by Will earlier." He turned to his brother, who took it from there.

"Cameras caught Daddy dearest going through customs at Toronto International Airport four days ago. We have him at different locations in the city before he disappears. Kanan is using his contacts on the ground there to find out where he might be hiding. The problem we have is Frederick knows how we think, so we need to think outside the box on this one boys and girl."

Will had a very different relationship with their father than Jack. He always had and seemed hardened to it or was used to the man letting him down and betraying him, while Jack was still struggling to come to terms with that.

Jack turned back to the team. "Thanks, Will. As you know, we don't know why or when or even how but we know his end game is to eliminate the Queen. Perhaps we need to work some different angles, but until we get home, the priority is to protect the Queen and get through this tour, not to go after Frederick."

"What about the Ravelino Cartel? Where do they fit into this?" Nate asked.

Nate was a good man and crack shot with a sniper rifle. He would be a good pick for the walkabout, and Jack made a note to speak to Zack about it.

"I believe I can shed more light on that, Jack."

He watched Astrid stand and face the room, her spine straight despite the tension he could see on her face. It took everything in him not to go to her and offer his support.

"I had a run-in with the cartel a few years back, and it's me they're coming for."

Smithy sat forward, resting his elbows on his spread knees, his hands dangling between them in a relaxed pose that belied the threat he was to those that hurt his family, and Smithy considered every person in this room family. "What do they want?"

Astrid faced Smithy with an outward calm, but somehow Jack knew this was hard for her. Without conscious thought, he moved closer to her, causing Lopez' eyes to widen slightly.

"Me, or rather information they believe I have."

"Do you?" Decker asked with a tilt of his head.

"No. I wish I did but I don't."

"This is very cloak and dagger. I feel like we're missing something here." Zin stood and walked to the outside of the room as he spoke.

"That's enough. You don't need the details to do your jobs." Jack's voice was sharp as he shut the questioning down. He felt a hand on his arm and looked down to see Astrid touching him. He looked into her face that brought out every protective instinct he had—and he had a lot—to see her eyes soften as a smile of reassurance tipped the corners of her lips.

"It's okay, Jack. They deserve to know."

He turned as if the eyes of the entire room weren't on him and spoke low, so only she could hear. "No, they don't. Not if you don't want them to. This is yours to decide."

"I know, and I appreciate your concern, but they need to know what we're facing."

He nodded and stepped aside for her to continue.

Her head held high, his firefly faced the men ready to fight to protect and keep innocents safe. "In my past life, I had a sister who was involved with the cartel through her job. My superiors told me that someone killed her. When I went undercover at the cartel, I found evidence that maybe she wasn't dead and was, instead, in hiding. I started digging and can only assume I left tracks."

Astrid swallowed, and he knew this was harder than she was letting anyone else believe. "I think they're after my sister, but I don't know where she is or if she's even alive."

Smithy glanced up. "But you think she is?"

"Yes, I do."

"Then we go with that theory." Zack glanced at him with a knowing look which he ignored. "This job, was it for who I think it was?"

Astrid nodded.

"Fucking pricks."

Jack couldn't disagree, and it was only from a few of the words

Astrid had used over the years that he'd realised she was former CIA before she told him. He guessed the same could be said for the rest of the men here.

"Astrid, let me have all the intel you have, and I'll find out how they found you and see if I can uncover any information relating to your sister."

Astrid turned back to the screen where Will was speaking. "Thank you."

The rest of the briefing was short and concise; the main objective was still to protect the Royal family after all, and Jack had no intention of failing. He had a meeting with Fitz next, and wouldn't have time to walk Astrid back to her room. She was talking to Blake, so he walked that way.

"Tell Pax to send me a picture, immediately." Astrid was smiling wide as if she hadn't just bore her soul to a room full of men. Perhaps she didn't understand what she'd revealed, but every man in here had read the nuance in her wording about her work for the cartel and what she must have gone through. Nobody came out of the CIA unscathed.

Blake chuckled. "I'll tell her."

"What's up?"

"Blake bought Pax a puppy." The delight on her face was addictive and drew him in like a moth to a damn flame.

Jack looked at Blake with a raised brow. "You got it after?"

"Come on, as if she was going to let me walk out without one after you told her about them."

Jack smirked. "They needed homes and I wanted them to have good ones."

"Wait, you know about this?" Astrid pointed between them waving her finger around.

"Sure, he does. He's the fucker that set me up."

Jack saw the confusion on Astrid's face. "My mum breeds Pomeranians and one of her girls had a litter a few weeks ago."

Astrid's face froze and she dropped her head on a snort before the rest of the laugh barrelled its way free. Her hand across her middle, she pointed at Blake. "*Oh. My. God.* I can't wait to see you walking a handbag dog."

"Yeah, yeah. Laugh it up but wait till you see Jack walking one. Now that's fucking funny."

"Fuck off, Blake. I was helping my mother out."

"Whatever. It was still as funny as fuck."

Astrid rolled her lips between her teeth as she tried to hold back her hilarity, and he shook his head and rolled his finger in the air. "Come on, get it out so I can go back to work."

She let it free, and he basked in the fact he'd made her smile, even if it was at his expense. *He was so fucked.*

CHAPTER TWELVE

SHE HADN'T REALISED that it would be so hectic in Toronto but was glad it was, or she would've gone out of her mind with boredom and worry. Ever since the attack, she'd felt a cloud looming over her, waiting for something to happen. At this point, she wasn't sure if she'd prefer that. She could deal with a situation happening, but the axe hanging over her head left a gnarly knot in her belly.

She hadn't had to attend the dinner with the Prime Minister so had spent the evening with Bebe going over what they knew of Adeline's last movements, which wasn't a lot and what they did have was hazy. The hospital opening had gone well if somewhat emotionally. Seeing the patients who would get the care they needed and hearing the families' stories made her tear up.

It made her want to call her own parents just to talk to them, but that was harder now she knew her sister could be alive. She could potentially fix their grief if she only worked harder and found the link, but it had been three years since she'd escaped Iago and she still had nothing.

Her head held high as she accepted another bouquet of flowers from a little girl for the Queen with a smile, Astrid glanced around the crowded streets. This was a logistics nightmare. No wonder Jack was so uptight half the time. Keeping the Monarch safe when tall buildings and hundreds of people surrounded them was like counting grains of sand—almost impossible to do and yet he still worked his butt off to do it.

It was safe to say her attraction to Jack grew with each passing day. Watching him with his men and his friends only added to that. He was more than the handsome package she'd lusted over for the last year or so. That was the thing she'd have to watch out for. Keeping her heart safe from that part of Jack would be tricky.

He was two steps behind the Queen as they carried on walking the street and one behind her. Blake was between the Monarch and the crowd in case anyone got overzealous and tried to grab at Queen Lydia or touch her in any way. Waggs was to his left with Mitch. Gunner was to the left side, and Liam and Decker were walking out in front. Alex was lost in the crowd somewhere and she couldn't see him. The local police force provided crowd control, but the police weren't there for the Queen's protection—they were.

They were as protected as humanly possible with extra coverage on the roof from Nate and Zack, who were watching through scopes. Will was monitoring the cameras, yet she still felt the tension radiating from Jack and his team as if they sensed something. She felt it too, but everything seemed as it should be as she continued to smile and take flowers.

The wind whipped at her skirt, and she dropped her hand to hold the flowy fabric down, the air cooler than previous days but the Queen and the Prince Consort didn't seem to notice. Although the Prince Consort didn't seem to notice a lot except his Queen, and she loved the way he stayed a step behind her, his hand at her back showing more about his feelings than a grand gesture would.

They were getting to the end of the street where they would cross to the other side and walk back down towards the cars. This was the dangerous part because crossing the wide road would expose them. As she'd been schooled by Alex over and over, she kept close as she handed off the flowers to someone who would deliver them to the local hospital.

Shouts from the mostly positive crowd filled her ears. An oddly negative comment penetrated and she briefly turned in that direction looking for a threat before turning back, not wanting her attention drawn away.

Halfway across the road, she heard a pop of gunfire and dove towards the Queen, but before she could reach her Jack had pushed her to the ground. The next round came with a grunt from the man holding her, telling Astrid it had hit him.

"Get Wilma out of here." His voice was muffled as he pressed her into the ground. "Find the shooter, Nate."

Screams from the crowd filled the air as the police tried to keep control of people panicking when what had happened sunk in and the threat to their own life, no matter how small, filled them with adrenaline.

Bile and panic squeezed her tight as Jack shouted into his comms. A group of men in suits broke off as the royal car sped towards them and Eidolon got the Queen safely into it before it sped away with Blake at the wheel.

The weight on her back released and she felt Jack take her arm and haul her to her feet and against his body as he looked around.

Blood was pouring down his jacket from his shoulder, but he didn't seem to notice it as he barked orders at someone through the comms. A second car appeared, and she saw Liam driving as the door flew open and Jack pushed her inside. She turned, panicked that he'd leave her, a sense of fear she'd never felt before filling her as she grabbed for his arm.

His eyes moved over her as he got in beside her, and the car was moving before the door closed.

"You're bleeding."

Jack looked at his arm and winced as if only just realising he'd been hit.

Liam looked at them in the rear-view mirror. "You need a hospital, boss?"

Jack shook his head, but she could see by the lines around his mouth that he was in pain. "No, it's just a scratch. Waggs can take care of it." His hand took hers and squeezed lightly. "Are you okay?"

Her eyes bugged. "Me? Yes, I'm fine. I'm not the one bleeding."

His eyes twinkled, and his lips twitched as if he wanted to smile, which at a time like this was ridiculous. "Worried about me, firefly?"

"No."

They both knew she was lying, so she turned the tables. "Why did you throw your body over mine? The Queen is the priority, not me."

Jack's jaw tensed, and a lethal look came over his features. "Not to me, it seems."

Astrid didn't push him on that. He'd shown more than he ever had how he felt about her with that one action, which could've cost him his life. He liked her at least a little bit, and it was more than the sex they'd yet to have.

He pressed his comms and cocked his head as if he were listening and she saw his eyes move to Liam before turning to her. "The Queen is secure and Nate took out the shooter."

"That's good. Do we know who it is?"

"Not yet, but my team will find out. Fortis is going to make sure the Royal family is safe while we run point on this."

"You're still bleeding, you know."

His thumb rubbed over her pulse. "I know, firefly, and Waggs will fix me up back at the hotel."

They remained silent until they got back to the hotel where Waggs met them. Jack never let go of her hand as they went up in the lift to the top floor and walked towards Jack's room where Waggs would meet them after grabbing everything he needed to treat Jack. She had no clue if they'd try and kick her out, but there was no way she was going. A base part of her needed to be close to him, to see for herself that he was really okay despite the bullet hole suggesting otherwise.

Astrid had seen her fair share of blood and gore, from bullet wounds to knife wounds and everything in between and it never got to her, but this one did. She was having a hard time not throwing up or passing out.

Jack sat on the couch, and she scooted into the other side giving Waggs room to work as he cut the ruined jacket and shirt away. Her eyes couldn't seem to leave the wound, which was oozing blood down the muscular bicep that had saved her.

That was why this was different; this bullet had been intended for her and Jack jumping in front of it meant he could have died to save her. Waggs continued to work, but Jack's eyes were on her.

"Astrid?"

Her head felt light as she stared at the broad chest covered with spatters of blood, an inch over in either direction, and his body could be sitting cold in the morgue. She swallowed, her breathing coming fast as she stood abruptly and backed away.

Waggs was suturing the wound now and covering it with gauze.

"Firefly? Where are you going?"

Her eyes shot to Jack as he stood, ignoring Waggs who grunted something at him. Tears hit her eyes and cotton seemed to fill her ears as she moved away from the reality, not wanting to face it.

Jack stepped towards her, and she found herself in his arms, surrounded by his scent now tainted by the smell of blood. His mouth at her ear. "Talk to me, firefly. Tell me what you're thinking."

Her body shook, and she knew it was adrenaline leaving her body, but it was more than that, it was the abject fear that Jack could have died and how she felt about that. This, whatever it was between them, was bigger than she'd thought—at least on her side. She should pull away, run from the truth today had revealed but she didn't, she stood in his arms and shook.

She heard the door click and realised Waggs had left the room.

Jack lifted her in his arms, and she let out a squeak. "Jack, your shoulder."

"Will be fine." He carried her to his bed and placed her in the middle, coming to lie beside her and gathering her into his arms. The sheets smelled like him, clean and fresh like the ocean with woodsy undertones that made her think of their date. Her head rested on his good shoulder, his hand rested on her hip, holding her body flush to his, and she could hear the steady beat of his heart.

"Tell me what's going on in your head."

It was such a simple question, yet the answer was anything but. "I don't know."

"Yes, you do, Astrid."

"You could've died." Her voice shook on the last word, and she had to pull in air through her nose to keep the panic from consuming her.

"But I didn't."

"But you could have, Jack. You shouldn't have done that."

"I'm finding I'm doing a lot of things I shouldn't do when you're around, firefly, but that wasn't one of them. When I heard that shot, it wasn't even a conscious choice. I just knew I had to protect you and, news flash, I would do it again and again."

"Why?" She knew she was blatantly fishing but needed to know.

"Because despite not wanting you there, you seem to have found your way under my skin. In that second, Astrid, I couldn't breathe for the fear that you'd been shot. Nothing else mattered. Not the Queen or the job, only you."

She smiled against his chest, her lips brushing the warm, naked skin. "You like me."

"I already told you that." He sounded a little grumpy, and she looked up as he dropped his chin to look at her, his eyes warm and expressive.

"No, you like me, like me."

"I have no idea what you're talking about."

His lips twitched acknowledging the lie he told her as his lips captured hers in a deep kiss that drove the terror and panic from her body, replacing it with lust and something she wasn't willing to accept. He rolled her so she was pinned beneath him and she welcomed the weight of his hard body pressed to her. The evidence of his desire for her pushed into her where she needed relief the most. His hand swept down her hip and up her thigh, pushing the silky fabric of her long skirt up, the callouses on his hands from the work he did lighting up her skin with need.

His tongue licked at her lips, and she opened for him, loving the way Jack kissed her, as if it was his sole focus and not as a means to an end as some men did. He seemed to be in no hurry to move things along, just enjoying his mouth and hands on her, but Astrid felt an ache build between her legs.

The need to feel his hands and mouth on other places on her body grew with every swipe of his tongue until she was a mass of writhing desire against him. "Jack, please, I need you." Her hands ran over his chest, feeling the slight tickle of hair under her fingertips, the ridges of muscle she wanted to taste.

"What do you need, firefly?"

Her hands smoothed over his abdomen, and felt his belly quiver as he growled against her lips, which was the hottest thing she'd ever heard. Her fingers clutched at his belt, and he pressed against her, trapping her fingers from moving.

"No. If you touch me now, my control will be shot and this will be over."

Her retort died in her throat as he rolled partially off her, his fingers finding the band of her panties, sliding under the edge and skimming her pussy lips before he moved his thumb directly over her clit and rolled, forcing her head to hit the pillow behind her and her eyes to close.

"Open your eyes, Astrid."

She forced her eyes open as he continued to drive her closer to the edge with his fingers. His free hand pressed into her lower belly as his fingers pushed into her and curled as they rubbed against the sensitive spot, sending her over the edge. Her climax pulsed through her on a wave of pleasure so consuming she felt her whole body jerk.

Jack held her eyes which contained a dark, stormy intensity that wrapped around her, and she knew she'd been right—this man could devastate her, but it was too late. She wasn't prepared to walk away now without finding out what it could be.

Her breathing finally settled and, as if her mind was coming back from a faraway place, she remembered Jack's shoulder. She sat up fast, almost hitting him in the face before he dodged out of the way, gasping between his teeth.

"Oh my God, I'm so selfish. You got shot saving me, and you end up soothing me and making me, well, you know..."

His lips twitched as he sat up on the bed. "Made you what?"

Astrid scowled at him as she straightened her skirt. "You know what."

"Yeah, I'd say from the flush over your skin, everyone will."

"Jack," she warned as she swung her legs to the floor and watched him stand and grab a shirt from a hanger in the wardrobe. Standing, she moved to help him put it on, sliding his shoulder into the fabric and doing the buttons up for him as he rested his hands lightly on her hips.

"For the record, that wasn't selfish, that was fucking spectacular."

"Yeah, well, I can't deny that, but you got nothing from it."

"Oh, I definitely got something. I got to watch you come, and that's the best medicine I've ever had. That vision, the memory of your breathy sounds in my ear, and the taste of your lips will sustain me for the rest of the day until I can do it again."

"Confident, aren't we?" She was teasing, he had every right to be confident at this point. She felt like she was a sure thing.

His lips skimmed her neck, finding her pulse and sucking gently, not enough to leave a mark but enough to drive her crazy. "I want you in my bed, Astrid."

She tried not to let the fact he only said bed disappoint her. He'd been nothing but honest from the start it was all he was offering. "Okay, Jack."

She kissed his lips as a knock on the door came, and he took her hand.

"Time to find out what happened."

CHAPTER THIRTEEN

"What the fuck was that?" Jack was at the front of the room, seated beside Astrid. He wanted her within touching distance, not willing to let her out of his sight for even a second. The image in his mind of the first bullet hitting the ground so close to her had his stomach churning. One split second, and she could've been gone, stolen away from him before he'd even had the chance to explore what was between them, and with each passing second, he knew it was more than sex.

His world had stopped turning for that moment in time, and nothing else had mattered to him but protecting her. He didn't know how or when it had happened, but Astrid had wormed her way into his heart and was setting up for the long haul. Yet, instead of anger or denial, he was at peace with it. This was right, she was right. They fit, and he felt slightly blindsided by it.

Alex leaned against the wall with his arms crossed and Jack could see Alex was as angry as he was. In fact, as he looked around the room, it was clear the entire team was furious it had happened. Each man took their job seriously, and failure was a personal insult.

"Nate took down the shooter, and we're working on an ID for him now."

"Actually, I have an ID." Lopez turned the laptop so everyone could see the screen. "Craig Miles was a former Marine. He was medically discharged three years ago after insurgents ambushed his team and his friends were killed. He's thirty-six, divorced, no kids, and blames the military and government for what happened."

"So he's a mercenary looking for revenge?" Liam spat, his distaste evident in his tone.

"Yeah, looks like and he had a bank transfer wired to him six hours before the hit for twenty grand."

"Can we trace it?" Jack wanted this sorted so he could tell the Queen the threat was eliminated.

"I'm working on that now."

"Get Will to help. I need this guy locked down before I meet Fitz in the morning."

"On it, boss." Lopez began typing and was quickly lost in his own world.

"Could this be linked to Ravelino?"

Jack twisted to look at Astrid. He still had her scent on his body, and it was a teasing reminder of what he'd rather be doing, which was new for him. A workaholic his whole life, he'd always willingly chosen work over everything else, but now he was finding he wanted to just be with Astrid.

"It's possible but there hasn't been any chatter since we took Iago and his men into custody. My guess is Ravelino thinks they died because that's what we put out for them to find."

"And what is the truth?"

Jack eyed Alex, weighing up his decision. It was his alone to make, and he knew that, but it was also his responsibility to keep his people safe. Alex made no comment making it clear this was up to him.

"A team escorted them back to the UK where we'll question them when we return." He knew that was vague and that Astrid had more questions, but she didn't voice them, just nodded. He could see the disappointment in her eyes, practically feel her pulling away from him.

"It's also possible, and in fact more probable, that it's linked to Frederick and his agenda. So, let's explore that too." His men got up and began the task of investigating this disaster. Jack flexed his fingers, the pain relief Waggs had administered to remove the bullet and stitch him up was wearing off and his shoulder ached like a bitch. No matter what the movies said, getting shot hurt like a motherfucker.

"You should rest."

He glanced at Astrid, seizing an opportunity. "Only if you keep me company."

She bit her lip, making his dick harden at the most inappropriate time. "I need to talk to Bebe."

"We can stop on our way back to my room. I could really do with a hand getting my shirt off and into the shower."

Astrid raised a perfectly arched, blonde brow. "Really, Jack? Does that ever work for you?"

He leaned in, taking a lock of hair between his fingers. "Never tried before, you tell me?"

"No, I don't suppose you ever have to try, Jack. Women probably fall at your feet willingly."

His lips twitched, wanting to smile but he was fairly sure he'd get a slap for his efforts if he did. "Are you jealous, firefly?"

A blush cruised her high cheeks bones. "Don't talk garbage, Jack. Of course I'm not."

"I am. The thought of any other man touching you before me makes me murderous."

Astrid stood abruptly, and he wondered if he'd pushed it too far too fast.

"You'd better get over that quickly then." She held her hand out to him, and he grinned as he took it and let her pull him up. "Come on, let's go update Bebe. We also need some food, and after I *might* help you with your shower situation."

Jack kept hold of her hand as they walked to her room and let themselves inside. It still looked like a whirlwind had been through, but it didn't bother him so much this time as it had the first time he'd witnessed it.

Astrid knocked on the adjoining door. "Bebe, it's me."

It opened immediately, and he watched the two friends embrace.

Bebe pulled away and ran her eyes over Astrid. "Jesus, you scared the crap out of me."

"I'm fine." She turned towards him with a beaming smile that made him want to kiss her. "Jack got in the way of me and the bullet."

"Thank God he did."

Jack acknowledged the unsaid words when Bebe looked at him with a nod. He hadn't done it for anyone else but Astrid, the thought of her not breathing gave him chills.

"I thought I'd check in with you and see what you found out?"

"Not a lot, but I know Juan Ravelino is at his home in Mexico, and it's all quiet."

"And how do we know this?"

"Because you're one of us and the second Roz heard someone attacked you, she pulled Mustique and Laverne in and sent them to Mexico."

"She shouldn't have done that. This is my mess."

"Hey!"

"No!"

Both Jack and Bebe started to speak, and Bebe let him go first with a knowing grin but he didn't care. He wouldn't have her blaming herself for any of this. Jack strode forward, his hand reaching for Astrid and pulling her against his body, surprised when she came so easily.

"Don't blame yourself. This isn't your mess as you put it, this is on Ravelino and what happened with Adeline. It's natural you'd go looking for your sister. God knows I chased Will across the world when he went off half-cocked to save Aubrey, and I'd do it again because he's my brother and I love him. Of course you'd look for Adeline."

She looked up at him her eyes twinkling. "Does Will know how lucky he is to have you?"

Jack pursed his lips and shook his head sadly. "No, and I try and tell him at least once a day, too."

Astrid laughed, and he felt the tightness in his chest loosen. "Idiot."

Bebe pointed a thumb back towards her room. "As that's out of the way, I'll get back to work. I have a few leads to follow up, and I'm meeting an informant later."

"You need back-up?" Jack didn't like the idea of anyone working this alone, and it had nothing to with their sex. He knew the women of Zenobi were easily as deadly as his men, not least because people never saw it coming with them.

"No, this one is a little jumpy, so if I show up with back-up, he'll run."

"Are you sure?"

"Yes, now go rest, and I assume tomorrow is as planned?"

"Not sure. I meet with Fitz in the morning, and we'll decide."

"Let me know."

Astrid grabbed some stuff and shoved it in a bag before they made their way back to his room down the hall.

Jack used the key card and cleared the room with Astrid beside him, her own weapon drawn. He liked that she was as dangerous and confident as he was. Something about a strong woman was attractive to him, but it didn't stop him from wanting to take care of her, which was new.

Normally he found that part of a relationship exhausting, the constant need to think about someone else and consider their feelings. Still, with Astrid, it was coming naturally, and they weren't even in a relationship. The truth was he didn't know what they were, just that it was important to him in a way nothing that had come before had been. Was it love? Not yet, but he could see it going that way very easily.

Astrid dumped her bag on the floor in the middle of the room and turned, flopping on the bed. "What do you want to eat?"

"Not bothered as long as it has meat."

Astrid cocked her head. "Neanderthal."

Jack laughed. "No, I just like my protein and it's good for healing."

"Is that a scientific fact or a Jack fact?"

He sat beside her, his shoulder bumping hers. "Is there a difference?"

"Um, I'm thinking not in your world." She grabbed the room service menu from the table across the room and paced towards him as she looked through it. "How about steak and fries?"

"How about steak and new potatoes and we can share some chocolate cake?"

"Jack, something you should know about me before this, whatever this is, goes any further and it's that I *do not* share chocolate cake. Ever."

He tugged her hand until she was standing in front of him, wincing when his shoulder protested but not caring, he wanted her close. Her scent teased him, and he knew the only reason he'd let Aubrey leave that damned scented candle at his place last time she visited was that it reminded him of Astrid.

"Good to know, but I feel I need to set things straight about my expectations from you."

Astrid shook her head. "No, you don't, Jack. I get it. You made it clear it's just sex, nothing more, and I have no expectations of anything else." She tried to put space between them by pulling away, so they weren't touching, but he wouldn't allow it.

"Will you let me get a word in edgewise?" He ran his hands up the back of her firm thighs, the skin supple and warm as her hands rested on his shoulders.

Astrid squinted her eyes and glared at him, and he knew he

needed to be quick, or he'd see some of the fire he loved directed towards him. "I don't do relationships. They take too much time. Invariably one wants more than the other, and someone ends up getting hurt or at the least, disappointed. I love my work. I enjoy what I do and in the past that's caused me issues, so I just stopped. In the last few days, I've found myself wishing work wasn't getting in the way of me spending time getting to know you better.

"I'm not proposing marriage or that we buy a house together, but I want more than sex, Astrid. I want time together having fun, doing nothing, talking, eating, and yes. Definitely having sex, especially as I know it will be mind-blowing."

She was silent, and he didn't know what else to say.

"Maybe we should discuss this after you eat? I don't want you making promises that you regret in the light of day, Jack. You're so much more than a pretty face and sexy body and I could easily let my heart get involved and end up hurt."

"I won't change my mind, Astrid, but if you need time, I'll give it to you."

She smiled the fake smile he hated and pulled away to order their food, including the cake. He wanted to get his hands on whoever had hurt her and wring their fucking necks. He didn't doubt in his mind some asshole had broken Astrid's heart, and the thought made him rage.

"Here, let's get you out of that shirt."

Her hands unbuttoned his shirt, and he willed his body to calm down, but it was no use. The picture in his head of her doing this for a very different result filled his mind. Her lips parted, and he could see she was feeling it too but now wasn't the time to move things any further. As much as he wanted that he also wanted her to feel secure with him, to know he wouldn't hurt her or allow anyone else to either.

His hand rested over hers, and he stilled the movements. "I've got it. You listen out for the food while I take a quick shower." He disappeared into the bathroom and locked the door, not sure if it was to stop her coming in or him getting out and taking her up on all she offered. He took a quick shower, making sure to keep his shoulder dry before he dried off and wrapped a towel around his waist.

Exiting the bathroom, he saw Astrid sitting at the foot of the bed. Her eyes skimmed over him, slowly taking everything in as she did. It took everything he had not to go to her and lay her back on the bed and finally taste her sweetness.

Instead, he crossed to his case, which was already packed ready to go and drew out a pair of grey sweats. Turning his back to her, he dropped the wet towel and pulled the joggers up his legs. He left his torso bare, not wanting the hassle of trying to get a shirt on when his arm already ached.

When he faced her again, a full flush of pink tinged her upper cheeks and he wanted to follow the line it took and see if she was that colour all over, but he resisted. "Want to watch a movie?" He rubbed the towel over his head, getting most of the droplets before he dropped it on the chair.

"I was going to do some research on the laptop and see if I can find out anything by going back and looking into my sister's early time before the Farm."

"Okay. Anything I can help you with?"

Astrid shook her head. "No, not really. I can do this in my own room if you like and let you rest."

Jack padded towards her on bare feet, and her eyes roved over his chest, stopping lower where the joggers rode his hips. His lips twitched with delight. "Eyes up here, firefly."

She looked guilty as she glanced up and straightened. "I'm not dead, Jack, and you can't walk around with all that on display and expect me not to look. How would you feel if I walked around half-naked?"

That mouth was going to get her into trouble one day, but he loved that part of her that had previously driven him crazy. "Firstly, don't mention you and dead in the same sentence again. It makes me rage, and secondly, if you walked around half-naked, I'd be walking around with my tongue hanging out and in a much worse state than I am now." He looked down to emphasise the boner he was now sporting and groaned when she sucked in a breath.

"That looks painful. You should probably fix that."

He looked at the ceiling. "God give me strength." A knock at the door was his salvation from making a move he shouldn't yet. "Can you get that for me, please?"

Astrid rolled her lips between her teeth, and he could see her trying not to laugh at his expense. "Sure."

"Payback is a bitch, firefly."

CHAPTER FOURTEEN

It had taken all her best intentions to sleep beside Jack the previous night without climbing him like a tree. She'd seen him without a shirt before. But wet from the shower and his feet bare, he was relaxed, and those joggers hid nothing, and there was a lot to see. A tingle ran through her, and she tried not to squirm in case she woke him but God, she wanted to. First though, she needed to process things and make sure he'd meant what he'd said.

She'd gotten her mind around it just being sex, but before she could indulge in all that deliciousness, he'd changed the goalposts on her, and she was thrown for a loop. On top of the man taking a damn bullet for her, it was a lot. A relationship with Jack was what she wanted, but it was more of a risk. He'd shown her sides of himself she hadn't expected. He was funny and kind and thoughtful and so sexy she could hardly think straight around him, and that was a huge draw, but it also made it so much easier to fall for him.

She eased out from under his arm, which was thrown over her belly, and was almost free when he opened an eye.

"Running away, firefly?"

Her spine stiffened. "No, I just have things to do."

Jack eyed her and rolled to his back, the expanse of his sexy torso on display. "What time is it?"

"It's early, only five-thirty."

Jack groaned and sat up on one elbow. "I need to meet Fitz in an hour and give him an update."

They had got word from Lopez late last night that Frederick Granger was linked to the dead shooter. It was a short-lived relief to know it wasn't because of her, but the pain it caused Jack made her want to get her hands on his father and kick his ass.

"Can I take the bathroom first?"

His sleepy eyes moved over her in a slow perusal, and she enjoyed seeing the predatory look in his eye. "It's gonna cost you."

Astrid placed her hands on her hips over her pyjama bottoms as she straightened away from the game of cat and mouse, causing a squirm in her belly. "What?"

"A kiss."

He was too much temptation lying in that bed like sin on a stick. "Fine." Astrid leaned in and pecked his warm and firm lips. It would be all too easy to sink into him.

She raced to the bathroom, grabbing her clothes on the way and locked the door. Jack was probably the deadliest man she knew under all that control, and it was his constant vice-like hold on his surroundings that had drawn her to him. She wanted to see him lose his cool, to show her the lethal hurricane she knew was beneath the veneer he showed the world, but that would take time. Luckily, thanks to him and his now wounded shoulder, she had that.

She took a quick shower, dressed in plain khaki trousers that were elegant and comfy and added a cream sleeveless blouse and a khaki jacket. She towel-dried her hair and plaited it before tucking it into a chignon. Ready to face Jack now she had her armour in place, she opened the door and almost jumped out of her skin when she found him on the other side, leaning against the jam as if he had all the time in the world.

"Jesus, Jack, give a girl some space."

He moved until his body was pressed against hers in the doorway. His steady blue eyes were boring into hers as he cupped her cheek. "I haven't changed my mind, and I'm not going to, so stop running."

His lips found hers, and he tasted of mint as if he'd brushed his teeth already. He kissed her thoroughly, his one hand curving over her hip and pulling her hard against his body, igniting the promise of more before he released her and pushed into the bathroom.

"Breakfast is on the way."

He shut the bathroom door leaving her to consider his words. Was she running? And could she trust his word? He'd never lied to her unless she counted him keeping the details of where Iago and his men were taken from her. But after her initial butt hurt reaction, she'd unpacked it in her head and come to realise that things were too new for him to just spill all of Eidolon's secrets to her. He had men he needed to keep safe, and caution was a good thing. Maybe her own caution would've stopped the shitstorm she was in right now.

Breakfast was delivered just as Jack came out of the shower, thankfully dressed in his usual suit and white shirt, at least usual for this tour. She couldn't deny he looked hot in a suit, but he looked hotter in full tactical gear in her opinion. They ate eggs and bacon with fruit and drank coffee, both knowing that the day would be long with the travel and they may not eat again until that night.

Astrid glanced at Jack over the rim of her coffee cup as she crossed her legs at the small table overlooking downtown Toronto. "So, I was thinking maybe when we get to the next hotel we could share a room."

"You ready to believe me now?"

"I guess."

Jack reached for her across the table, pulling her to her feet then down to sit across his lap. His hand fisted in her hair, knocking the chignon free. "That's fucking fantastic news, and I promise I'll always be honest with you, Astrid. I can't promise work won't be an issue or that I won't fuck up, but I want this. For the first time in my adult life I want more. I want you."

"Me too, Jack."

"One day you'll tell me who hurt you." His jaw was like steel, and a tic in his eyebrow showed his anger, but his voice and touch were gentle.

"You gonna hunt them down, Jack?"

"You want me to I will." His thumb grazed her cheekbone, and she felt a Jack sized void opening up in her heart. He was a good man, and the thought anyone could hurt him made her so angry.

"He isn't worth it, and that's a story for another time, so get your hiney up, or Fitz will be banging on the door."

The mild-mannered James Fitzgerald, known to them as Fitz, was a stickler for details. Everything had to be in place when and where it should be, so yesterday would have sent him into a melt-down. She knew while she'd worked on uncovering her sister's past in the hopes it would uncover her present, Jack had been responding to email after email from Fitz.

"Let's go then. Make sure you're packed and ready to go by eleven."

He grabbed his bag and swept his eyes around the room before placing his hand on her back and walking her out. He walked her to her room and kissed her lightly, not caring who saw them. Astrid blushed when she saw Blake raise his eye brows behind Jack's back as he stepped out of the room he was sharing with Liam.

"Didn't know it was bring your girlfriend to work day, Jack."

Jack kept his eyes on her as he grinned. "Yeah, I forgot to hit send on the email. Sorry, Blake."

Blake laughed as he walked past.

"Is that what I am, Jack? Your girlfriend?"

"You are as far as I'm concerned but if that doesn't suit you, call us whatever you want. Make no mistake though, you're mine now, Astrid."

A shiver went through her at the dominant way he claimed her but gave her back control in the same moment. "Girlfriend suits me."

He leaned in and gave her another peck on the lips. "Good."

He walked away down the hall, and she watched until he turned the corner winking at her as he did. She thought her heart would beat out of her chest or she might swoon like in the movies. That was too much gorgeousness right there, and she may not survive but what a way to go.

She was barely through the door when her phone rang, the caller display showing Roz's number. Astrid picked up. "Hey."

"Are you kidding me? Sleeping with the fucking enemy, Astrid?"

Astrid walked to the end of the bed and sat. "Don't be dramatic, Roz. Jack isn't the enemy, and for the record, I haven't slept with him yet."

"Pax said that Blake said he called you his girlfriend."

"He did. We're seeing each other."

"But you haven't had sex yet?"

"No."

"Isn't that like buying a car without a test drive?"

Astrid couldn't stop the grin at Roz's words. "Really, Roz? You think with all that intensity Jack would be garbage between the sheets? Plus, if he fucks like he kisses, I can assure you that a test drive is unnecessary. In fact, for that analogy, it would be like buying a Lamborghini. You don't need to drive it to know that it has some serious power under the hood."

"Yeah, I guess so, and he might be an ass, but he is kinda hot." Roz and Jack had a complex relationship that thrived on mutual dislike and respect for each other. "But if he hurts you, tell him I'll carve out his heart with a rusty knife and feed it to him."

"Don't let K hear you say that." Astrid heard a baby cry in the background. "Is that my favourite boy?"

"It is. He's teething which is hell on earth for both of us. I kinda hate K right now for leaving me."

"You could never hate him, and we both know it."

"Uh-huh."

"How are the girls?"

"Fine, both killing it in school."

"I miss them, tell them I'll bring them something back."

"The only thing we want back in one piece is you, so be careful."

"I will and thanks for sending Bebe to have my back."

Roz snorted. "Sounds like Jack has your back and front. Mustique says everything is quiet at the Ravelino villa."

"Good and thanks for that too. I don't know what I would do without you."

She didn't either. Zenobi had come into her life at her lowest point and built her up and helped her heal. They'd then given her a purpose, a focus, and she loved them all like sisters. It wasn't the same as Adeline, but it helped.

"Any intel on Adeline?"

"No, but my guess is they think I have some, so maybe that means I'm on the right track."

"Okay, I need to go to work. We have a disgusting human being who thinks it's okay to beat his wife and daughters almost to death on the daily. He's about to find out that it most certainly is not."

"Okay, talk later, Roz."

"Bye, Astrid, and stay safe. Call if you need anything."

"I will."

Astrid hung up and smiled. Zenobi was her family, but Jack could just maybe be her future and having Roz not taking a gun to his head would be a good thing.

The door to her room flung open and Bebe looked at her with excitement. "I have a lead."

Astrid jumped up and moved towards her friend. "What is it?"

"A sighting of a woman who looks like your sister."

Bebe showed Astrid a grainy image that could be Adeline, but her hair was short now, and she couldn't be sure, but any lead was something.

"Where was this taken?"

"That's the best bit. Montreal."

Adrenaline zipped through her blood at the thought of her sister possibly being so close.

"My contact said he'd meet us at four-thirty this afternoon but only us, so we can't tell Eidolon."

Astrid bit her lip knowing Jack wouldn't like it, but she had no choice. This wasn't something she could give up, and she was no ordinary woman. She could handle herself and any situation she found herself in and so could Bebe. "Fine."

She might regret this, but Jack would have to learn that she was who she was and much as she wanted to be with him, she wouldn't change or bow to pressure from a man ever again—not even him.

CHAPTER FIFTEEN

Jack turned as the door to the room they were using a base for the Montreal operations opened and Fitz walked inside. He'd wanted to cancel the tour, deeming it too dangerous, but the line from the Palace was that it would continue unless there were any further incidents. So here they were in another hotel. The only good thing about the day was at least he was guaranteed to see Astrid today at some point because they were sharing a room.

That hadn't gone over particularly well with Fitz either, who'd said it compromised her place at the Queen's side. Jack had agreed that the rooms would stay on paper as they were, with Astrid and her female security officer—Bebe—sharing adjoining rooms and Jack having his own room. Still, in reality, he and Bebe had swapped, with him taking the adjacent room and her having his room.

The team were all aware of the change, but anyone on the outside wouldn't be.

"What do you need, Fitz?"

"I wanted to give you the details of who will be at the school tomorrow so you can check things out."

Fitz handed him a piece of paper, and Jack scanned the names, not seeing anything that stood out. "Fine, I'll have Lopez go over it."

He knew he was being curt but didn't have the energy in him to do anything else. Part of it was guilt eating away at him knowing his father was the cause. Last night he'd again offered his resignation which was flatly refused.

Fitz sighed and leaned against the desk Jack was working at, undoing his suit jacket. "Look, Jack, I know this isn't easy for the team and especially you, but we all have a job to do. Mine is to make sure the Queen is protected. In a different way from you, sure, but I still have to see her best interests and her requests are carried out. For her, the most important thing is to be seen, to serve her people. I know that makes things difficult in light of things, but we know if anyone can keep her safe it's you and your team."

Jack scrubbed his hands down his face, the move making his stitches pull, reminding him of what could go wrong. "One inch either way and we'd be having a very different conversation now, Fitz."

"I know, which is why we've agreed to cancel the public walka-bouts and only attend the small events that can be managed."

Jack looked up at the man he'd been working with for years now and respected, as much for his iron will as he damned it. "Even those come with risks."

"Her Majesty is aware and understands the risks are hers to take."

"Then we'll do our job and make sure she stays safe."

Fitz nodded as he stood and rebuttoned his suit. "Thank you, Jack."

It was rare for the man at the Queen's side to show thanks and even rarer for him to say it, so Jack took the peace offering for what it was. He looked down at the list as Waggs, Lopez, and Liam followed Kanan and Zin into the room.

Waggs placed a covered plate in front of Jack. "Brought you some food, boss man."

"Thanks, Waggs, but I'm a big boy, you know. I'm perfectly capable of getting my own food."

"Yeah, well, it wasn't my idea. Astrid asked me to make sure you ate."

"She did?"

Jack couldn't hide the twitch of his lips at the thought of her worrying about him. He lifted the lid and saw chicken tikka kebabs and roasted Mediterranean veg. His mouth watered and he looked at his watch seeing it was already five o'clock. He shoved the piece of paper towards Lopez as he bit into the flavoursome meat. "This is the list for tomorrow. Have them checked out."

"Bit late in the fucking day, isn't it?"

"Yeah, but we work with what we have."

Lopez was working long hours trying to track down all the leads on Ravelino that might lead to Adeline as well as doing all the work for the tour. Thank God Will had taken over the search for Frederick.

He couldn't even think of the man who had sired him without wanting to hit something. That he was somehow now in bed with Ravelino was fucked up. It was like he was going after Astrid to weaken Jack and the team and split their focus. Fuck, that *was* what he was doing.

"Waggs, is Astrid in her room?"

Waggs shook his head. "No, she and Bebe went out to meet a contact."

Jack stood abruptly, the food forgotten as ice-cold fear clamped around his throat. "Are you fucking kidding me?"

The men in the room paused as if sensing his mood change and that the slightest thing might tip him over the edge.

"No."

"Find her." He pointed at Lopez and stalked from the room. He'd forgotten this part of the woman he was involved with. The reckless, wild side that drove him crazy, even while it drew him to her in a way that was hard to understand.

He made it to the lobby of the hotel, the lift opening into a grand entrance, yet he saw none of it. He didn't know where to start because she hadn't fucking shared her plans with him. His strides were long and determined as he made it to the door and looked up and down the street lined with paparazzi.

He felt a presence beside him and turned to see Reid walking alongside him.

Lopez's voice came over the comms. *"I have her and Bebe leaving the hotel via the side and going towards town."*

Jack was already walking in that direction and trying and failing to keep his calm. When he found her, they were going to be having words about her keeping shit from him. Secrets were what got him into this mess in the first place, and he had no place in his life for any more. Then he was going to make it clear how much she meant to him by fucking her until she had no energy left in her body to go off on a wild goose chase.

"Okay, go right at the end of this street and follow it to the end. She and Bebe just went into a bar."

Jack broke into a jog as their surroundings got dicier by the second. He could feel eyes on him and Reid and none of them were friendly. What was she thinking coming here without protection? Reid kept pace beside him, and if it wasn't for the fact they both looked mean as fuck, God knew what would've happened.

He saw the sign for a strip joint but no other building. "Lopez, is this the place?"

"Yes."

He turned to Reid. "Watch your back in there."

Jack ducked his head as he went through the door into the dark, dingy room with neon lights around the door. Stairs led down to a large open space with a stage near the front where a young woman was dancing in a barely-there bikini. A few men watched and tried to touch, but a burly bouncer kept watch and stopped any attempts they made.

To his left was a bar where a few patrons sat and was lit by the same neon lights. His eyes skimmed over the room, looking for the one person who could rattle him more than any other. His gaze stopped on two dark heads in the corner of the room. The lighting made it hard to see them as they wore dark clothes, but he'd know the tilt of those shoulders anywhere.

With a single-minded focus, he stalked towards them. His hand landed on the back of Astrid's neck as Bebe's eyes in front of him went wide.

"Hello, firefly. I didn't realise we had a date planned tonight." He sat down beside Astrid, who to her credit looked contrite, a high flush on her cheeks, her full lips open in surprise. Reid sat beside Bebe, making it seem as if this was a normal evening.

His hand banded around her waist as he pulled her close, his lips feathering over her ear as she shivered in what he knew wasn't fear but hunger for him. "What the fuck is going on?"

Astrid turned slightly as if she was nuzzling his neck. "I got a lead on Adeline."

His body stiffened, and he knew he had to let her have this. They would definitely talk about the how, but now he was there, and she was somewhat safe, he felt his calm return, and his heart beat return to normal. "We're gonna talk about this later."

Her fingers speared through his hair, and she ran her lips over his ear, making him want to take her to the ground and make her scream his name as she came apart under his hands and mouth. "I would expect nothing else, but for now, you're probably scaring off my contact so can you go do your fretting from the bar?"

"I do not fret."

"Totally fretting." She kissed him then, stealing his reason, and he pulled away, not wanting his focus split when it came to her safety.

"Reid, let's get a drink." Jack stood, and he and Reid walked to the bar where they ordered a beer and sat so they could both watch the room and the exits. They waited for an hour until Bebe went stiff, her shoulders losing their relaxed pose as she looked at her phone.

Jack went to stand as Astrid dropped her head in silent defeat before straightening. That was his girl, the one who didn't let anything beat her, who took the blow and got back up and it was fucking irresistible.

They walked to him, and she didn't need to say anything for him to know that something bad had happened. A wrinkle of guilt swept over him, but he shut it down, he didn't care about anything but her safety.

"Our contact is dead."

He cupped the back of her head. "I'm sorry."

Her arm tucked into his, she burrowed closer, the hair of her wig whispering over his cheek and he missed the blonde that was so vibrant and alive. "Let's get back to the hotel before anyone sees us."

They walked quickly back to the hotel, going in through the side and avoiding the photographers camped at the front. The four of them took the lift up to the fifth floor and exited.

"I'm sorry, Astrid. I thought this guy would come through."

Astrid let him go and moved to Bebe, gripping her upper arms. "This isn't on you, and I love you for helping me." The two women hugged, and he waited as Reid went back towards the room they were using as a base, to no doubt update the rest of the team.

"I need to find out what happened to him. He didn't deserve to die for helping us, plus I need to figure out how he was made."

"My men will help you with that, and reach out to Will. He can help you."

Bebe looked at him and nodded. "Thank you."

"But for God's sake, update your boss first. I don't want her breathing down my neck accusing me of trying to steal her team members again."

"Yes, I will."

"I should probably check in too."

Astrid wouldn't meet his eyes now. It was as if she finally realised there'd be repercussions for her actions, but he had no intention of causing a scene. The Royal Suite was four rooms away from where they were, and Blake and Dane stood outside the door watching them quietly.

"That can wait. We need to talk." He gripped her upper arm and steered her towards the room he was using, pushing her inside before closing and locking the door. With a deep breath, he turned to find her standing in the middle of the room, her back to the bed, her foot-tapping, her arms crossed.

"You can't push me around, Jack. I'm not scared of you."

"Oh, you should be, but not because I would ever lay a finger on you in anger, firefly, but because by the time I next leave this room, you'll be so exhausted from the pleasure I give you that standing long enough to get into more trouble won't be an issue."

CHAPTER SIXTEEN

Astrid faced down an angry Jack knowing there would be blowback for keeping things from him but never in her wildest dreams had she expected the words that came out of his mouth. Her breath hitched and her heart began to pound as desire and need so strong it felt like a physical touch hit her, almost buckling her legs. But they never got a chance because the second the words left his lips he was prowling towards her, and she found herself retreating until the backs of her knees hit the bed and he was on her.

His big, solid body took her down to the bed, one hand cupping the curve of her ass, the other shoving the wig from her head as if it offended him. His fingers flexed on her scalp as he gripped her, his lips slammed into hers, hard and angry and desperate. She got a taste of the man she knew was underneath the veneer.

A moan pushed past her lips as she held on to his hips which he pressed against hers, the evidence of his desire hard and unrelenting like the man himself. His mouth moved to her ear, and she arched her neck, wanting his hands on her everywhere. His fingers dug into her ass cheek before smoothing up her belly and over her collar bone to her throat.

He wrapped a hand lightly around her neck, his thumb rubbing over her pulse, which was wild, starving for his touch. "You scared me, firefly. I don't scare easy, but the thought of you out on the street with no back up fucking undid me."

"Jack."

"No, you had your chance to speak, and you didn't take it. You kept things from me, and I won't tolerate it. I can't do this if you hide and lie. I just don't have it in me, Astrid."

Guilt was warring with desire now, making her regret the burden she'd added to his shoulders and the already heavy load he carried. He was responsible for everyone and was being betrayed by people who should love and protect him, and she'd added to that for her own selfish reasons.

His eyes met hers, and she saw the storm, the demons he fought and the hunger for her that she'd never seen before, not on him or anyone else. She knew in that second she was falling in love with him, that she'd do anything to stop his pain including giving up her own control.

"I'm sorry, Jack."

He didn't answer her, but his lips dropped to hers, and he kissed her, his tongue stroking over hers, mastering her, until she was consumed by him. He lifted his head long enough to push her jacket off her shoulders and pull the blouse over her head. His eyes devoured her as if this was the first time he was seeing her, when he'd already seen more at the beach.

Her own hands tugged at the shirt he wore, pulling it from his trousers so she could feel the warm skin of his abdomen under her hands. Jack moved his hips, knocking her legs further apart so she cradled his hips between her legs. His hard cock pushed harder against the fabric that separated them and sent a sensation of pleasure rocketing down her spine.

Jack pulled the straps of her bra down each shoulder before unhooking it with a flick of his wrist and tossing it to the floor. His mouth found her nipple, and he sucked deep, making her body arch and her fingers grasp at his head, holding him to her as her legs clamped around his waist. She came with a moan as he rocked against her, his mouth on her nipple.

The ceiling blurred, and her eyes rolled back in her head as her body contracted and pulsed with pleasure. Jack lifted his head and gave her a killer smile. Astrid saw the challenge in his eyes and never one to back down from anything, rolled until he was on his back. He had a glint in his ice-blue eyes that seemed to warm with fire.

She straddled his hips, the heat of his cock pulsed against her and the tingle of her body from her climax made her feel powerful, yet relaxed. The edge being taken off her need allowed her to take her time. Her hands unbuttoned his shirt, separating the white cotton and allowing her to see all of him, the white of the bandage at his shoulder causing her belly to clench in regret.

"Eyes on me, firefly." Instantly she answered the command in his tone and brought her eyes to him. "Touch me, Astrid. I want to feel your hands on me like I imagined so many times before."

"You imagined this?" Her voice was husky, heavy with lust.

"Oh so many times."

His words were like a caress to her confidence. She'd never been meek or mild, always outgoing, but even on her best days, Jack wanting her had seemed like a distant dream.

Her hands skated over his belly, a finger finding the dip where his eight-pack met in the middle before she tipped forward, wanting to run her tongue along it. His mouth caught her breast as she did, and he sucked her nipple, making all her intentions leave her brain as she let sensations overwhelm her.

Forcing her body to pull away from the sinful touch, she smiled. "My turn, remember?"

Jack placed his hands behind his head, giving her the illusion of freedom when they both knew he could have her on her back in an instant. Bending again, she let her tongue trail his neck, flicking at his nipple which made his hips buck underneath her before she swept it down the length of his chest, all the way to the edge of his trousers.

"You're killing me, Astrid."

Her smile was one of victory as she slid the button of his slacks through the hole before dragging the zipper slowly down. Pushing the fabric away, her hand gripped his cock through the white cotton boxer briefs and squeezed, forcing a growl from his throat that caused slick and hot desire to wash over her, making her clench her legs together in an involuntary action to ease the ache he'd created with just a sound.

Bending her head, she freed his cock. The strength and feel of it in her hand had her swallowing hard as her hand stroked, following the slight curve over the head that was wet with pre-cum. Her tongue flicked out, and she tasted the salty liquid surrounded by the scent of him, musky and heady.

"*Fuck*. I wish you could see how beautiful you are, Astrid."

His hand reached down to cup her cheek, holding her hair out of his way so he could watch her lips cover the crown before taking him deep, the soft skin covering the hard cock was a dichotomy, and she loved it. Gripping the base, she stroked his cock as she bobbed her head. Jack's hips bucked as she felt his control begin to slip free of the tight hold he kept on it. She wanted that; she wanted his feral side, the side he tried to contain.

He was still trying to rein in that rigid control, holding on to it as if he was afraid to let go and she wanted him to. Redoubling her efforts, she swirled her tongue over the underside of his cock before hollowing her cheeks.

"Fucking hell, firefly, that feels so good. You're gonna make me come."

Astrid wanted that, to make him feel like she did when he touched her, to know that she had the same power he did. Moaning around his cock, she felt the ache building in her pussy. She'd never been so turned on by going down on a man, but this was different. It was so much more than the act itself, it was about trust, and he was giving her some of his true self.

The hand on her hair tightened and his hips bucked as he fought for control. As she felt him pulse inside her mouth, she looked up and found his eyes on her. Eyes the colour of a stormy sea, with so much darkness that she was sucked in until she tasted his release and still, he held her eyes as she swallowed, licking up every drop as she released his still hard length.

Before she could react, he had her on her back, his body looming over her half-naked one. "You're perfect, you know that? Beautiful and full of fire, kind and gentle but with so much strength. I could stay in this room with you for days, years even, and not get enough."

"That sounds exhausting." Astrid stroked her fingertips over his stubbled chin.

"It does, doesn't it? And yet I want it like a drug. I don't know what you did to me, firefly, but you're making me your slave."

Astrid's brows rose, not at what he'd said, because she understood that perfectly, feeling the same way. It was him admitting it to her and making himself vulnerable that surprised her the most. "Is it wise to tell me that?"

His teeth grazed her lip, tugging gently on the flesh as his cock, which was still hard, ground against her. "Time will tell."

Then there were no more words as he stood and bent to pull the jeans she'd worn to the bar off, taking her underwear with them. Her shoes had been lost ages ago, kicked off in the heat of their need for each other. As he stood back and surveyed her body like she was a fine antique, precious and delicate, he stripped. Dropping his shirt to the floor before he lost his trousers and boxers.

Jack watching her with naked hunger in his eyes as he fisted his hard cock sent a rush of wetness to her pussy. An almost unbearable ache to feel all of him hit her.

"On your knees, firefly." The command was full of desire, and she scrambled to turn over, pushing up onto her knees and watching him over her shoulder. Jack had sheathed his cock and now gripped her hip with one hand as he lined the head up with her slit. He swiped his cock through the wetness, and she shivered at the touch.

"So, fucking wet for me, Astrid."

"Hurry up, Jack."

His smirk was dirty and sexy as he ran his hand over her spine and pushed inside. It wasn't fast, but it was by no means slow either, and she felt the fullness as he stretched her. Jack paused for a second before he began to move, fucking her slow and steady as he gripped her hips hard enough to leave marks she knew would be a beautiful reminder of what they had shared.

"You're so tight. We fit like we were made for each other."

His words hit home, and she couldn't help thinking that was because they were, but then his hand found her pussy, his finger stroking over her clit and all thought was gone. Her legs began to shake as her climax built from the way his cock stroked over that spot inside her, the sensations flooding her body and she knew this was going to be so much more than she'd experienced before.

Her hand reached back for him, she needed to hold on to something.

His hand bandied around her belly, holding her as he continued his assault on her senses. "I've got you, firefly, let go."

His words were like a release, and a long sob caught in her throat as her body peaked and spasmed, every nerve seeming to come alive as she came so hard her vision went white. As she came down Jack pulled out and she wanted to cry at the loss, but he gently lifted and turned her to her back before smiling down at her and re-entering her body.

This position afforded her the luxury of watching his handsome, brutal strength as he moved inside her. The muscles of his biceps bunched as sweat beaded his skin and she held onto his butt cheeks. Her legs tangled with his and he moved faster, chasing his own release as he built a second one from her.

It crashed over her like a gentle wave this time, and she was able to experience the beauty of Jack as he came on a groan that made her sex clench. His body sank into hers, and she welcomed the weight of him, holding him close, her arms wrapped tight around him.

"Jack."

His head lifted, and sated eyes found hers. "Hum?"

"If that was a deterrent, it was a huge failure because I'm pretty sure I'd do just about anything to have that every day."

He kissed her lips. "That wasn't the deterrent, firefly. Not getting it was."

"Oh." Her fingers played with the hair at his neck. "Jack?"

"Right here, beautiful."

"That was life-changing."

"I know."

"You do?"

"Yes, because now I won't let you go. Not ever."

Astrid let that settle over her, feeling a peace that until then had eluded her all her life. This was what she'd been missing.

CHAPTER SEVENTEEN

JACK HAD NEVER FELT anything like he had the night before with Astrid. He hadn't lied when he'd told her it was life-changing. The second he'd entered her body, he'd known that whatever happened from here on out, he needed her by his side. She was the missing piece that soothed the part of him that prowled with an unleashed edge, that was continually telling him he wasn't good enough.

He didn't need a shrink to tell him it was a part of him he couldn't control, that he was still looking to prove he was good enough to earn the pride of a man who would never give it. Some part of him still strove to be the best, to show his father he was worthy. Yet his conscious mind knew it was his father who was unworthy, not him.

He felt like that man with Astrid. A man who was worthy of pride and who wanted to do better; not for validation from his sire but for her and the people he cared about. They were what counted, he knew that, had always known that but now he could feel it too. The need for revenge didn't gnaw at his insides; now it was justice he sought. Retribution for what his father had done and putting a target on the woman Jack found himself thinking about day and night.

He straightened as the door to the Royal Suite opened, and the Queen emerged. "Ma'am."

She nodded her head. "Jack. Is all well?"

"Yes, ma'am, the car is waiting."

"Lead the way."

Jack got into position beside the Queen as Astrid fell in step behind her. He couldn't say he was happy that Astrid was still putting herself in the line of fire, but this was the job he'd asked of her. To put a stop to it now that they were together was an insult to her professionalism and skill. He wanted to, he wanted to lock her up somewhere safe where she wouldn't risk a bullet, but he knew from dealing with Aubrey that wouldn't go over well.

Reaching the lobby, he looked around and found his men had already cleared the area and were now positioning themselves so the Queen had full body protection until she got into the car with the Prince Consort, Astrid, and Blake.

Astrid wore a cream pleated skirt that fell to her shins with brown heeled boots and a tweed jacket and scarf. He knew she was armed and that slightly mollified him, but she had no protective clothing under her own because as thin as the armour Will had designed was, it was still visible and would blow her cover.

As the door closed on the car, he saw her offer him a small smile of reassurance which lodged in his heart. He was in the second car with Liam and Gunner. Waggs, Mitch, and Decker were ahead of them. Lopez would monitor the feeds from the base. Will had tapped into the traffic cameras and kept an eye out, looking for any unusual activity. Zack and his team had gone ahead to the school to make sure all was clear.

Liam side-eyed him as he drove. "You and Astrid, then?"

Jack nodded. "Yup." He didn't want to get into this with them, not now or ever to be fair, but he knew he wouldn't get out of it.

"About time."

Gunner reached forward, and fist-bumped Liam. "Amen to that."

"What the hell does that mean?"

"Oh, come on. You two have been dancing around each other for over a year now."

"No, we haven't."

Liam raised his brows at Jack. "Uh, yes, you have. Why do you think we all disappeared when she came over to train with us?"

"I have no idea."

"Because the sparks you two were throwing out almost set the building on fire."

"Rubbish." Jack glanced out of the window at the car ahead of them who held the most precious person in his life right now and wondered if things had been building for longer than he was willing to recognise.

"Whatever, boss man."

He sighed. "Was it really so obvious to everyone but me?"

Gunner nodded. "Yep." He slapped Jack on the shoulder and squeezed hard. "It's okay, boss. It takes some people longer than others to wake up, but you got there in the end."

Gunner was a blissful newlywed, while Liam and Taamira had just under a year under their belts, and both men had never been happier.

Jack had never considered marriage for himself; his own parents had a difficult one, and it had put him off. At least his mother had a hard time; his father had the life of Riley. He did what he wanted when he wanted, and still came home to a cooked meal and a warm bed. Frederick had never mistreated his mother, but he'd been selfish. He often wondered why his mother had stayed as long as she did but had never asked. Now she'd washed her hands of her husband after finding out the extent of his misdeeds, but Jack thought if he were going to reach out, it would be to her.

He should call her tonight and check in, make sure she was coping okay. His love for his mother was something else that was complex. She'd always tried to put herself between Frederick and her sons, to be the buffer, but he couldn't understand her staying with him when he'd put so much pressure on them.

He knew if he ever had children he'd encourage them to be whatever they wanted and would always make sure they knew how proud he was of every single accomplishment, no matter how small. That was new too. Kids had never been on his radar, but being with Astrid opened his mind to all the possibilities he'd never considered.

The car stopping pulled Jack from his thoughts as they came upon the school for special needs children. The building the Queen was opening was for a sensory suite that would allow the kids to explore things like touch, light, and sound in a way that was engaging for them.

The men's vibe changed as they got out and surrounded the Queen's car and waited for Blake to exit. Astrid came next with the Prince Consort, and lastly, the Queen, who looked calm and regal.

He moved in behind, keeping his distance as Fitz started the introductions to the school leaders just under the canopy. His eyes flitted around on constant alert, his adrenaline pumping enough to keep him focused. He watched Astrid shake hands as if she'd been doing this her entire life. Like she was a real lady in waiting for the Queen, and not an undercover protection officer.

As they made it inside, he watched her crouch in front of a child who was handing out flowers and offer a few words. The shy smile the little girl returned caused his heart to constrict with a feeling he didn't recognise and certainly wasn't ready to explore right then.

They walked through the new suite, and he was impressed with the way things worked, giving the children there a chance to interact in a way most people took for granted. His focus stayed on task watching for any movement or threat, but there was none.

They were gathered around the plaque as the Queen gave a speech about the work being done there, and Astrid was standing off to one side watching the crowd. Jack angled his body towards her, so he saw the second her spine went straight, as invisible as it was, and her face paled.

He glanced around looking for the source of her unease and saw nothing for a minute, and finally spotted the source of her unease as a woman who was shorter than Astrid with dark hair, turned away. He glanced back to the woman he'd come to know so well these last few days and saw her knuckles were white as they clenched at her sides. When he looked back, the woman was gone.

He fought with the urge to go after her, but it could be a trap, so he stayed in place. His eyes were on the woman he could see was in pain. All he wanted to do was help ease whatever was causing it and he couldn't.

As they moved off, he let his little finger graze hers. She hooked her finger around his for a second as if taking comfort in the secret gesture before it was lost and the distance was there again. Pressing his mic, he spoke low, so only Lopez could hear.

"I need eyes inside the school looking for a woman with dark hair, about five feet four. She left the sensory suite a few minutes ago. Find her."

"*On it.*" Lopez went quiet, and Jack focused on the job in front of him safe in the knowledge his team would find her.

"*Got her. She left the building out the back door and is heading east towards town.*"

"Track her. Do not lose her."

He didn't know for sure, but everything about Astrid's reaction told him that the woman was Adeline. If they could locate her, they might get some answers. As they made it through the tour, he kept a close eye on the room, reading the temperature of everyone in it and looking for any indication that there was a problem. He had to remember that while Astrid knew the woman her sister had been, she'd been assumed dead for four years which in itself made her an unknown.

He didn't like to think wrong of Adeline because he knew it would devastate Astrid, but he wouldn't compromise her safety by being stupid and trusting a woman he'd never met. There was a reason she'd disappeared, and until he knew what it was and what her intentions were, he wouldn't allow Astrid to become a pawn or a casualty in her game.

"Blake, change of plans. I'm in the car with Queen and you take my spot."

He waited for the pause, and then Blake confirmed. *"Roger that."*

Jack never changed a plan halfway through an assignment, but this was different. Astrid was hurting and he needed to be near her, to offer what he could in the way of comfort.

Jack stepped forward as Blake stepped back, and he caught the scent of Astrid's perfume, settling his anxiety over the situation they were in.

Fitz frowned as he helped the Queen into the car, followed by the Prince Consort, Astrid, and lastly him. He would want answers later as to what was happening, but Jack didn't care.

The door closed, and moments later the car began to move. He could feel the tension coming from Astrid, and knew his boss could too, as she looked at her with kind concern.

"Are you unwell, Astrid?"

Astrid blinked, her eyes moving from the Queen to him and then back again. "No, ma'am."

The Queen tipped her head. "Are you sure? You look like you saw a ghost."

Astrid dropped her head to her hands before looking back up. "I think I did, ma'am."

That was all the confirmation Jack needed to know he was on the right track.

"Perhaps Jack can make sure you get some rest this afternoon, and later, if you would be willing, there is something I wish to discuss with you. Perhaps over afternoon tea?"

Astrid nodded. "Of course, ma'am."

The Queen nodded. "Good. That's settled then."

The Queen laid her hands in her lap, gloves covering her skin, and he saw the Prince Consort lay his hand over hers and squeeze.

"No meddling, ducky."

The Queen gave him an affectionate look full of love and meaning, and one he'd rarely glimpsed between the couple who were so often guarded to the outside world. The intimacy they shared was just for their family to witness usually, and he understood the level of trust being bestowed on him and Astrid.

"Whatever do you mean?"

The Prince Consort shared a look with Jack, one that men who loved women the world over knew as loving acceptance that they wouldn't change the woman beside them despite the storm that swirled around them.

Jack wouldn't have recognised that a few weeks ago, probably not even a few days, but now he did because he loved a woman just like it. It was a startling realisation for him at a time when he was in the company of the most important woman in the world, and to him that was Astrid.

CHAPTER EIGHTEEN

THE SECOND she got into the room she was sharing with Jack, she felt her legs give way but his arms were there to catch her. She leaned into him as if he alone could keep her from shattering into a million pieces.

Seeing Adeline at the school had been wonderful and awful at the same time. Her body had gone cold, her blood seeming to freeze in her veins and her nerves tingled with the urge to rush up to her and throw her arms around the sister she'd believed to be dead.

The stark truth staring at her made all the years of pain seem meaningless. Her sister had just stared for a few moments, their eyes locked, a wealth of unanswered questions flying soundlessly between them. She'd been seconds away from breaking her cover and going to her, but the imperceptible shake of her sister's head had stopped her.

There was a reason her sister had chosen that place and time, knowing that Astrid would be surrounded by people and unable to act on seeing her without risking the lives of those around her. The thought made her angry, but that had given away to fear. It was confirmation that her sister was hiding or running from something, and the CIA had known about it or were possibly even involved with it.

A hand stroking her back brought her back to the present and the man who'd settled her with a slight touch and then switched up his team so that he could be close to her. He'd been the first person she'd wanted to turn to when she'd realised what was happening, and he'd instantly picked up on her emotions and acted on it.

"Did Lopez find her?"

Jack shook his head. "No, he lost her when she went towards the docks. I'm sorry."

Her hand rested on his arm. "Don't be. This isn't on you."

Standing, she felt the excess energy burning through her veins, threatening to drown her. Throwing her jacket off, she began to unbutton her blouse as she kicked off her boots. Her hand went to her zipper at the back of her skirt, and familiar hands stopped her.

"Let me, firefly." His lips found her neck, and she let her head fall forward as his body crowded hers. His hands moved over her and pushed the skirt away as if he knew what she needed. She was naked as he turned her to face him and something about him being fully clothed as he watched her, his eyes moving over every inch of her skin, made her shiver with anticipation.

"Spread your legs, Astrid."

She did as he said, her eyes following his movements as he dropped to his knees in front of her. The move made her feel powerful as she watched him grip her calves, pushing her leg so she had to spread them even further.

He kissed her thigh and the mound of her pussy before he swept a kiss over her needy clit, her body already heightened with pleasure from just this. His dominance, fused with the care he showed her, was heady.

His tongue came out to lap at her slit, making her head fall back and a whimper escaped her throat. His hands cupped her ass cheeks, his fingers digging tight as he held her up to keep her legs from buckling. His tongue speared inside her, lapping at the wetness of her desire for him and his touch, but she needed more.

"More, Jack."

He met her demand, his lips sealing over her clit as he sucked hard, her climax hitting her hard and fast and sucking the air from her lungs until she was panting. Dropping her head, she gazed at the man who'd given her so much already and held out her hand. He took it, and she pulled him to standing.

He came easily, and she placed her hand in the centre of his chest, pushing until he sat in the chair behind him. His forearms were resting on the arms of the easy chair like a King on his throne. He may have been on his knees for her just a moment ago, but she didn't doubt in her head that he was the one in control.

Her hands moved to his fly and she quickly unbuttoned it, exposing his hard cock to her eyes. She needed this, more than anything she had before, this release, this contact with him alone.

"I'm on the pill."

His blue hooded eyes found hers. "Are you sure?"

"Yes. I want nothing between us, Jack."

"I'm clean. I've never... not before."

His words were all she needed as she placed one knee on either side of his hips and sank onto his rigid length in a single movement. A growl moved through his chest as he threw his head back, his hands finding her hips and holding her still. Lifting his head slowly, he looked at her with reverence and passion, making her feel safe and loved. Rooted her in the moment when her entire existence felt like it was coming apart.

"Take what you need, Astrid."

Her body took over, fighting for the release she needed, her hips rising and falling on his length. The eroticism of him being fully clothed made her feel wild and free as she took and took until she was on the edge of another climax. Her eyes never left the man who was keeping her grounded, saving her from the grief and pain she knew would swallow her whole.

Lifting his hand, he cupped her nape, bringing her mouth down to his and kissing her, deep and slow. "So beautiful, my wild firefly."

"Jack, I want us to come together."

His eyes were liquid fire as he placed his hands on her hips and started to move, fucking her from below. "Touch yourself, Astrid. Play with that pretty pussy for me."

Her hand went to her centre, and she stroked her clit, the climax building as she felt the drag and slide of Jack's cock inside her and then she felt his mouth on her breast, the bite of his teeth on her nipple and followed by the soothing lap of his tongue. She came hard, her body clamping down and dragging his climax from him as he groaned against her skin and came. The heat of his release flooded her body as her arms came around him, holding tight to the only man who'd ever let her feel at peace and be herself, even when she didn't know who that was some days.

Jack stood with his cock still inside her and carried her to the bathroom and sat her on the counter, the ceramic cold on her bare skin.

Sweeping her hair from her face, he tipped her chin to look at him. "You okay, firefly?"

"I think so. It was a shock, and I feel so out of control like everything is coming at me so fast and I have no time to process before the next one."

He kissed her forehead. "What can I do?"

"You already did it, Jack. You gave me control and let me work through my energy."

Jack winked at her and her body clenched around his still hard cock. "I'm always here for you, Astrid, especially if that's how you work through your issues."

She smiled when an hour ago, she wanted to cry. "I mean it, Jack. You knew I needed you and let me take it. You're a special man."

He grinned at her as he withdrew his cock after two more strokes which made her moan in pleasure. "How about a shower and we go see what the team found before you meet with the Queen later?"

"Sounds good."

She watched him turn on the shower to a warm heat and strip naked, marvelling at the beauty of the man she was falling in love with. The warm spray hit her skin, bouncing off Jack's chest and running down his hard abs, and she felt the need to share some of her past with him.

"Have you ever been in love, Jack?"

He scrubbed the water from his face before looking at her. "Nope, never been in love." He picked up the shower puff and motioned for her to turn, which she did, letting him soap her back.

"I have, at least I thought I was."

She felt him freeze behind her before he continued. "What happened?"

"We worked together, and I thought it was perfect. He was older than me, but he said he loved me and even asked me to marry him, but I soon saw him for what he was and more importantly, who he was."

"Which was?"

"A liar, a fraud. He was my handler on the Ravelino case. He was the one who forced me to sleep with Iago. I knew then he didn't love me and was heartbroken, and I was so determined to prove I was worthy and do the job I became reckless. I think he was the one who burned me too."

"I'll fucking kill him."

Astrid looked over her shoulder and saw the fury in Jack's eyes and had no doubt he meant his words. Laying her hand on his chest, she shook her head. "He isn't worth it, and I don't even know if he's alive."

Jack cupped her cheeks in his hands. "If he is, I'll find him and kill the motherfucker for what he did to you. Nobody hurts what is mine."

"You're sweet, Jack. Do you know that?"

"Woman, stop with the sweet. Until a few weeks ago you thought

I was Satan and I thought you were a sexy vixen with a death wish. How can I go from that to sweet so fast?"

"Firstly, any man who walks a Pomeranian puppy for his mother is sweet, and secondly, I never thought you were Satan. I just thought you needed to chill a little and I think we accomplished that."

"Oh, is that right?" He gripped her ass and lifted her, the head of his cock against her entrance as she held onto his shoulders, aware of his healing wound. "Well, how about you walk the dog from now on and we work on keeping me chill with this special brand of therapy?"

He slid into her, his cock filling her, and she whimpered.

"Yes, that works for me."

All talk stopped as he made love to her slow and easy against the tiles. It was the first time in her life she knew the difference between fucking and making love.

CHAPTER NINETEEN

Jack didn't want to let Astrid's hand go as he walked into their base of operations at the hotel and saw his men turn to look at them. After what she'd told him and what they'd just shared, he was undoubtedly halfway in love with her already, if not all the way there.

They walked straight to Lopez, who was working on his laptop, which was attached to multiple screens. "What we got, Lopez?"

He glanced up and looked at Astrid as if seeing her for the first time before pulling his gaze away with a frown. "Not a lot. We lost Adeline when she hit the dock area, and I haven't been able to pick her up since. I'm running facial to see if I can find her, but I suspect if she's stayed hidden for so long, then the chances are we won't find her."

Jack agreed. Adeline hadn't been there by accident. She'd come with the sole purpose of seeing and being seen but what was her game? He held up his hand and beckoned his team closer.

"We need to brainstorm this and figure out how it's all linked, and I know it is somehow." He sat in a chair and Astrid sat beside him, her thigh touching his as he let go of her hand to take the coffee Alex handed them both.

"Thanks, Alex."

Jack watched Astrid smile at his second and couldn't help the feeling that everything would be okay as long as he had her with him. She had, in a very short period of time, become everything to him. The thought should scare him, but it didn't in the least. Maybe it was because she knew his secrets and the strain of the job and understood them or perhaps it was that he'd finally met the one everybody talked about.

"You want me to dial Will in on this?" Lopez asked.

Jack shook his head. "No, let him sleep. The Queen is secure with Mitch and Reid watching her and Fortis will need to remain sharp tonight with everything going on. We know that was Adeline at the school, but we need to know why she was there and how she links to Ravelino and Frederick."

He glanced at Astrid, looking for any sign of pain and found none, just focus. After what she'd told him about her ex-boyfriend and what he'd done, he'd rather cut off his arm than hurt her. He'd meant what he'd said though. When he'd finished with Frederick, he was tracking that fucker down and putting a bullet in his head. Vermin like that didn't deserve to live, and he had no problem with pest control.

"The Ravelino link is me and the picture I found in Juan's room."

All eyes turned to Astrid.

Jack cocked his head. "You think this all goes back to that first mission?"

"Yes, it has to. I was looking for my sister, and Iago and his men show up, then my sister makes an appearance."

"That makes sense."

Alex sipped his espresso as he nodded his agreement. "What about Frederick though? He links to the Ravelino cartel but how does he know about your sister?"

Astrid got up and began to pace as she bit on her thumbnail, before spinning to face them. "What if he has no idea about Adeline?"

Liam crossed his arms over his chest as he leaned against the desk. "I don't follow."

"Okay, let me show you." Astrid grabbed a black marker and went to the whiteboard they used for formation planning. Flipping to a clean page, she wrote down Ravelino, Frederick, and Adeline at the top and then her name, CIA, and Eidolon at the bottom.

"Okay, so Frederick links to you and Ravelino." She drew in the lines as she spoke. "I link to Ravelino, you, the CIA, and Adeline. Adeline links to me, Ravelino, and the CIA." She kept drawing until it was a tangled web and he was frowning, a headache forming in the back of his eyes at the thought of his father.

"I think Frederick went to Ravelino purely because he found a link to me and my failed mission. By attacking me, he destabilises you."

Gunner smoothed a hand over his long hair, his hatred for Frederick almost as strong as Jack's over what he'd done to him. "So, you don't think he knows about Adeline?"

"No."

"That makes sense. He never mentioned any ties to the CIA or the cartel, and I'm sure he would've utilised both before now if he had them."

"So, Frederick alerted the cartel to where we were in the hope they would attack Astrid and force us onto the back foot?" Jack was catching up to her thought process now.

She beamed at him. "Yes."

"Okay, I get that but why would that force Adeline out of hiding and what does she want?"

"That I don't know yet. I do know she wanted me to see her but not be able to follow her, which was why she picked that place and time."

Jack glanced at Alex. "Have Shadow find out from Iago if this lines up. I want to know how he found Astrid and what he knows."

Astrid raised a brow. "Shadow?"

Jack and his team were the only people who knew about Shadow Elite and he needed it to stay that way. A team like the one he'd assembled needed to work in total darkness to function the way he needed them to. Fortis and Zenobi couldn't know about them, but she was there, and if they were going to create a life together he'd have to be honest with her, even if that meant being honest about the fact he couldn't tell her.

"Can we talk about this later?"

"Yes, of course. Or not at all if that's better for my mental health."

Jack shook his head. "No, we'll talk. Just not now."

"Whatever you need."

"Okay, back to the subject at hand. Let's operate on the premise that Frederick is still playing his own agenda and Ravelino isn't an issue for the moment. Do we have any sightings of him anywhere?"

"No, he's laying low, but we'll find him. I have every programme known to man, and a lot that aren't, running, and they'll flag any sighting or mention of his name."

Lopez was watching Astrid again, and Jack didn't like it. He needed to find out what the issue was if there was one. They'd all been working around the clock the last week and needed to get some sleep. "Okay, everyone, tonight I want you to get some sleep and let Fortis handle things. People are starting to look burned out, and that means mistakes we can't afford."

Blake chuckled. "Sleep, Jack? Is that what we're calling it now?"

"Yeah, well, enjoy it while you can because I hear you won't be having much in your future."

Blake gave him the finger and Astrid frowned as she looked between the men. "No way! Is Pax pregnant?"

Blake glared at Jack. "Thanks, asshole."

Jack shrugged but remained silent.

"Yes, she is, but it's early days, so keep your mouth shut about it."

"Blake, watch how you speak to her." He loved Blake like a brother, but he wouldn't tolerate anyone speaking to Astrid like that.

"It's fine, Jack. He didn't mean it."

Blake folded his arms. "No, I didn't, and I'm sorry." He eyed Jack. "Next time though, maybe keep my private life private."

Alex slung his arm over Blake's shoulder and knuckled his head, hard. "We're family. We don't have boundaries and congrats, man. Evelyn will be happy to have someone in this with her."

"She already has Autumn with them both due so close together."

Alex paled a little, and Jack fought the urge to laugh at his friend's terror. "I know, and it's only ten weeks to go. It's scary and exciting."

Jack loved to see his men so happy and becoming fathers, and he knew he'd do whatever it took to make sure they were around for those babies.

Astrid grinned at Waggs. "What about you, Waggs? You want more kids?"

Waggs held his hands up. "Wow, hold up. I haven't got a ring on Willow's finger yet, and we have already one that I'm still figuring out."

"He's adorable, though."

She turned to Liam, who stepped back as he pointed a hand at Jack. "Jack, control your woman before she jinxes us all. I want Taamira and I to keep practising for a while before we jump on that wagon."

Astrid laughed as Jack hooked her around the waist and brought her close for a kiss. He would never get enough of this woman, and a child with her sounded like something he'd like one day. "I could never control her, and I don't want to. She's perfect as she is."

"Ah, Jack, that's so..."

He placed a finger over her lips. "Don't say it, firefly."

She smirked and went to bite his finger, but he pulled it away and kissed her again.

"Get a room you two. Not everyone can have their girlfriend on the tour with them and it's making us all feel like sad, heartsick losers."

Jack pulled away and grinned at Liam. "Fine, keep me updated. I need to meet with Fitz about tomorrow."

Lopez and Decker had already wandered off when the talk moved to babies.

"Sure thing, boss man."

Jack walked beside Astrid as they left the room. "What time is your meeting with the Queen?"

She checked her watch. "An hour but I want to change first."

"Okay. Let me walk you to our room before I meet Fitz."

She looked at him shyly, and he realised how wrong he'd been about her. She had a wild streak, but it wasn't a death wish as he'd thought. She wasn't the reckless woman he'd perceived her to be. Oh, she had her moments, but he'd underestimated her in so many ways, and he felt guilty for it now.

"Why are you frowning again?"

He looked up, his eyes raised in surprise. "Was I?"

Her finger stroked the crease between his brow as they stopped at the door of the room they shared. "Yes."

"I was just thinking how wrong I was about you. I thought you were out of control, had a death wish, but I was so wrong. I'm sorry about that, Astrid, I really am. Maybe if I'd opened my eyes and stopped being such a blind fool, we'd have found this sooner."

Astrid shook her head. "Don't be sorry, I wore that persona like an armour, still do in a lot of ways."

"Not for me."

"No, Jack, not for you ever again. You make me feel safe without it."

"You will always be safe with me, firefly. I would give my life for yours."

"I hope we never have to find out, but I feel the same way." Her lips met his in a quick kiss. "Now go before I drag you back to bed and show you how much those words mean to me."

"Rain check?"

"Absolutely, handsome."

Jack left her at her door and went to meet with Fitz. When he arrived, the man was waiting with his leather-bound notebook in his hand. They spent the next fifty minutes going over plans until Fitz took a call.

He glanced up at Jack as he did, and Jack tensed for more bad news. "What?"

"The Queen would like you to join her and Astrid for afternoon tea."

Jack closed his phone where he'd been making notes. "Do you know what this is about?"

Fitz shook his head. "I do not, no. I do know Her Majesty is rather taken with Astrid."

"Aren't we all?"

"Mmm, it seems that way."

Jack checked his watch and the two men walked out of the room Fitz was using and down the hallway towards the room he unofficially shared with Astrid. He stopped and knocked, and she opened in seconds, a surprised look on her face at seeing him. Bebe standing behind her like a watchdog soothed his soul a little at the knowledge she was protected by those around her when he wasn't there.

"Jack, what are you doing here? I was just leaving for my meeting."

"It seems I have an invite now, too."

Astrid took his arm, the pinch between her eyebrows showing she was as curious as he was. She dressed in a pale pink fitted dress with a bow at the waist and some sort of cape over her shoulders. She looked stunning with her hair down and around her shoulders, just the one side pinned back. He was wearing his usual for the tour, which was a suit and shirt with a tie. He had to look the part at all times, but he hated it and couldn't wait to get back into combats and t-shirts, and he knew his men felt the same.

"I wonder what this is about." She glanced past him at Fitz, who shook his head.

"Let's find out."

They stopped outside the Royal Suite where Reid and Mitch were standing guard, both alert and showing no emotion at seeing them there.

He nodded at his men and waited while Fitz went ahead before ushering them into the Queen's inner sanctum.

She stood and greeted them, Astrid dipping into a curtsey and he a bow before the Queen sat at a table set with finger sandwiches and tiny delicate pastries that Alex would love.

"Please do sit."

Jack held Astrid's chair out for her, and she sat before him as he settled next to her. Fitz poured tea for them all and stepped away to give them privacy. Jack understood he stayed in the room at the Queen's request. The Prince Consort wasn't in attendance, and he wondered where he might be until he stepped from the other room that also served as a study inside the suite.

The Queen looked at Astrid. "I'm sure you are curious as to why I asked you here."

"Yes, ma'am."

"The truth is I've grown fond of you over the weeks, Astrid, and greatly admire you as a fellow woman in a man's world. However, I fear you're hiding something from me, and I would like to know what it is that troubles you."

Astrid looked over at him in panic, and he reached for her hand.

The Queen zeroed in on it immediately and nodded. "I can see I was correct in that at least. You're lovers. Am I correct?"

"We're more than that, ma'am." He wanted to tell the Monarch he loved Astrid, that she was everything to him, but she deserved to hear it first. So, he gave the Queen what Astrid already knew. "I would die for her."

"I see," she turned to Astrid, "and you feel the same way?"

Astrid squeezed his hand. "I do."

"Good, this makes me happy."

"It does?" Jack was lost. He'd thought he was about to get fired because he'd basically admitted to fraternising on the job, and he knew it could compromise the Queen.

"Don't look so surprised. I like romance as much as the next woman and seeing two people I hold in high regard together makes me happy."

"Thank you."

"I see you're confused. I want to know why Astrid was so upset earlier."

Astrid again looked at him for answers, so he nodded for her to go ahead with whatever she wanted, and he'd support her. At least he was trying to convey all those things.

Astrid took a deep breath. "I saw my sister."

"Go on." Queen Lydia pushed the food forward, and Jack took a sandwich and plated one for Astrid.

"I thought my sister was dead. I was told she'd been killed four years ago but I suspected she was alive. She was at the school today."

"Oh my. Did she try and approach you?"

"No and she disappeared before I could speak to her."

"Why did you stay at your post instead of chasing her down? I know I would have been tempted to do so had it been me in that position."

"I won't lie. For a split second I considered it, but I was working. To have moved would have compromised your safety, so I stayed put."

Jack was so proud of her and wished he had her strength. He saw the Queen nod at her husband, who was quiet as always.

"And you, Jack? Did you notice this?"

"I did, ma'am, although I wasn't entirely sure who I saw. Just that it had upset Astrid."

"Did you wish to pursue her?"

"Yes, but as Astrid said, it would have compromised you, so I had Lopez track her."

"Did you find her?"

He shook his head. "No."

"I'm sorry about that."

"Oh, please, don't be sorry, ma'am. I'm sorry my personal life has affected you at all." Astrid went to reach out to soothe the Queen and stopped herself, realising what she was doing. Instead, the Queen reached for her hand and took it between hers.

"You and Jack have both demonstrated how loyal you are to me, and that you would give up the chance to see a loved one to keep me safe. For that, I thank you. I've discussed it with my husband, and we feel the tour should be cut short."

"Oh no, not because of me I hope?" Astrid looked panicked, and he leaned closer.

"No, my daughter is having some issues, which we discussed, and I feel it is best to postpone in light of that and return to the tour perhaps next year."

"Are you sure?"

Astrid and the Queen seemed to have a closer relationship than he'd realised, but he shouldn't be shocked. Astrid charmed everyone she met with her class, good humour, and candour.

"Yes, my dear. Now let us have tea so Fitz can get on with the task of cancelling my engagements."

Jack was a little stunned to be there having the conversation, but he was relieved he could now concentrate on finding both Adeline and Frederick.

CHAPTER TWENTY

Astrid sat up with a start at the same time Jack did, both reaching for the weapons they kept beside the bed. The slightest noise from the room next door had woken her. It wasn't a sound she could identify but, nevertheless, it was there. Jack motioned for her to get the door on his count, which meant he'd go in first and high and for her to go low.

On his count she flung the door wide, the light of the moon coming from the window catching on a dark shape already racing for the fire exit.

Jack turned to her. "Call Alex. I'm going after them."

She had no time to respond before Jack was gone, chasing after whoever had broken into the room which was, for all intents and purposes, the one she should be sleeping in. Clearing the room, she turned on the lights and went back to her room and called Alex.

As she wandered through, her gaze tagged on a piece of pink paper leaning against the lamp beside the bed. Her heart crashed into her chest as she recognised the same type of paper she and Adeline had used as girls to write secret notes to each other so their parents wouldn't catch on.

Sitting heavily on the bed she picked it up with shaky fingers and noted the long scrawl of her name on the front. As she was about to flip it open, the door crashed in, and she raised her weapon, pointing it at Alex and Gunner as they rushed inside.

"Is the Queen secure?"

Alex nodded. "Where did Jack go?" Alex was checking the room as if to reassure himself that the threat had left the building.

"He went after them, but he won't catch her." Astrid smiled, knowing how good Jack was but also knowing her sister would have had at least three or four escape routes planned before she even set foot in the hotel.

"Her?"

Gunner moved closer, and she looked up at him. "My sister. She left this." She held up the note for him to see. As she did, a movement behind her caught her attention, and she saw Jack come through the fire exit, not even breathing hard.

"I lost whoever it was in the alley behind the restaurants."

He looked pissed about it, and she looked at Alex with a raised brow. "Told you."

Jack looked between them as he moved towards her, his eyes going to the paper she held. "Told him what?"

Astrid passed him the sheet, and he took it trying to read her expression, but she didn't even know how she felt so she had no idea what her face told him. "That was my sister." She nodded at the paper in his hand. "She left that."

Jack turned it over. "What does it say?"

"I don't know. I'm scared to read it."

Jack turned to Alex and Gunner. "Clear the room. I'll be down shortly."

He turned back to her, hauling her into his arms, not seeming to question if his men would obey his order because he knew they would.

"She's reaching out, firefly, that has to be a good thing."

Astrid nodded. "Maybe but what if it's to tell me to let her go? I don't think I can do that."

His hand swept over her cheeks, pushing her sleep-rumpled hair off her face. "Then we'll find her and convince her otherwise."

"Okay, Jack."

"Good, now let's read this letter and whatever it says we'll face it together."

He handed it back to her, and she flipped the paper open and read the two lines.

Bumble, meet me at the last warehouse on the right beside the shoe factory at six am.

Love, Bee

Astrid gasped, happy tears filling her eyes as she glanced at Jack with a smile. "It's her. It's really her. Only Adeline called me that, it's from when we were kids."

"That's good, firefly."

His smile lit up his entire face, but she knew he was holding back and why.

"I know this has no promises of a happy ending, Jack, but I have to go and see her. She's my sister and I have to hope and believe it will work out."

"I would expect nothing less. If it were Will, I'd go in a heartbeat. I just don't want to see you hurt." His thumb stroked over her jaw, and she closed her eyes, enjoying the soothing touch and all the unsaid emotion behind it. "You mean a lot to me, Astrid. More than I ever thought possible."

"I know, and I feel it too, which is why I need to find her so I can move on to the next phase of my life."

Jack stood. "Let's get dressed and go see the guys. I need to find the hole in my security that your sister so easily highlighted too."

Astrid tugged the hem of Jack's t-shirt she'd worn to bed down, thankful that she'd worn it and he'd opted for sweats and a tee too, or everyone could've been left red-faced.

. . .

DRESSED IN FULL TACTICAL GEAR, including bulletproof clothing from head-to-toe, Astrid stood behind Jack as they came upon the warehouse where her sister had asked to meet her. Adeline hadn't said to come alone, but Astrid had convinced Jack to make sure Liam, Waggs, Zack, and Dane stayed back a little so as not to spook Adeline. He'd drawn the line at her going in by herself and was coming with her, especially after the team had discussed it and decided it could be a trap.

While it was most likely Adeline waiting for them, as Lopez had her on camera entering the district at two am which was just after she'd left the note, the CCTV stopped after that.

He'd tapped into the feed from the shoe factory, which caught the edge of the warehouse they were watching and was monitoring it. Unfortunately, it left the other side blind, which was a problem because although she knew her sister, a lot could change in four years.

"Do you see any movement?" Jack was leading the op. Even though it was her sister, he'd taken over and she was fine with that. His situational awareness was more precise, and she was compromised by emotion which could lead to mistakes none of them could afford.

"I have one heat signature inside the warehouse, but it isn't moving."

"It's time, Jack, we need to go." Her fingers gripped his waist and the steady warmth of his body was comforting.

"On my count."

Jack counted them in, and they were all moving. Zack, Dane and Liam went around the back and cleared that while she, Waggs, and Jack moved in from the front. It was quick and efficient with each man checking in as soon as a section was clear.

When they were all ready to go in, they did it as one to make sure no mistakes happened. The inside was dark with lots of storage containers and tall racks built on either side. Weapons out, Astrid and Jack methodically cleared each section before moving on. Her instinct had her desperate to run through to the office area where she knew the heat signature was, but sense, born of years of training with the CIA and more recently Zenobi, had her holding back and doing what was needed.

"*Clear,*" Zack called through the comms.

She caught sight of them as they converged on the office where there was no sign of movement or sound. Jack motioned for Zack, Dane, and Liam to stay back a little but indicated Waggs come with them and she knew what he was thinking. Her heart began to beat wildly with a sense of foreboding. Quickening her step, she felt Jack move in closer to her and Waggs flanked her left side as she'd seen them do many times with the Queen on this tour.

Stopping at the door they listened and with a nod from her, Jack breached the door. Her eyes searched frantically around the small room before landing on a crumpled body in the corner.

"No!" The pain in her chest squeezed tight as she ran, falling to her knees beside her sister.

Astrid felt horror fill her as she took in Adeline's injuries. Her face was barely recognisable she was so beaten and she had a bullet wound in her side which was bleeding sluggishly. Reaching for her neck, she felt for a pulse and almost fainted with relief when she found a shallow, thready one beating beneath her fingertips.

Her eyes caught Jack's. "I have a pulse."

Her hands moved to cover the wound but were brushed out of the way by Waggs. "Let me see to her."

The urgency in his voice clued her in to just how bad this was. She sat back on her knees and her hand trembled as she stroked her sister's dark hair, not knowing where else to touch in case she caused her more pain.

Waggs poured a clotting agent into the bullet wound while he began to assess Adeline's other injuries. He looked up at Jack. "We need a chopper if she's going to have any chance at all."

"On it."

Astrid prayed harder than she ever had in her life as she watched the men who'd come to mean so much to her work to save her sister. They'd come too close to getting her back to lose her now.

"Come on, Bee, you can fight this. I know you can. I won't let you die on me a second time."

Astrid carried on talking while Waggs stabilised her, talking nonsense and begging her to fight. The sound of a helicopter overhead made her look up and into the worried eyes of the man she loved. A man who was doing everything in his power to make sure she didn't lose her sister again. Neither one of them had said the words, but she knew she loved him and had a feeling—or maybe a hope—that he felt the same.

A gurney appeared along with two paramedics who moved Adeline as they fitted a line to get fluids and medications inside her. Waggs gave the two men everything he knew. As he cited the injuries he'd picked up on, Astrid felt the weight of the fight her sister had suffered almost take her legs from under her.

Jack was at her back, a strong arm banded around her waist holding her up. "We're coming with her."

The paramedic nodded. "But only two and you need to move."

As they rushed to the chopper, Jack gave Zack and his team orders on what he needed from them and issued a request they inform Fitz what had happened.

Astrid climbed in beside her sister, who was pale with her oxygen saturations dropping. The aircraft lifted off, and she held tight as a headset was placed on her head by Jack, who was still bolstering her, his arm around her as she watched, helpless to help.

They were nearly at the hospital when her sister coded.

"She's hypoxic, and her blood pressure is dropping. We're losing her."

The paramedic placed paddles on Adeline's chest, and Astrid began to cry, the thought of her sister dying more than she could bear. "Don't die, Addie. I need you."

Jack held her tighter, and she let him take the weight of her pain, knowing he could take it.

. . .

HOURS after her sister had been rushed through to surgery, Astrid was still waiting for the doctor to come and find her. The waiting room was full of people who cared about her. Bebe had shown up the second she'd heard, her arms going around her friend and holding tight, along with all the available men from Eidolon and Fortis.

"She'll be okay, Astrid. I know it."

Bebe hadn't left her side except to get coffee for them all. Jack had been a constant presence, not leaving her alone for a moment. Waggs had shown up with Lopez, who'd immediately sat down, taken out his laptop, and got to work.

Kanan had come too, and she knew it was because of Roz. His big arms wrapped around her as he kissed her head. "Whatever happens, Astrid, we've got you, okay? You're family, and we're here for you."

"Thanks, K."

She curled back up next to Jack, her head on his chest, not sleeping, just waiting and remembering all the things she could about Adeline. The way Addie hated having her hair cut, the fact she'd spend hours reading when Astrid wanted to play outside. She'd missed her so much, but in the middle of all her anguish, she found solace in the fact that she had people around her who would hold her up when she was down and a man who would catch her when she fell.

She lifted her head to look at him handsome in full tactical gear, with scruff on his strong jawline but softness in his eyes which held hers. "Thank you, Jack."

"You don't have to ever thank me for being here for you, firefly. There's nowhere else I would be."

"I love you, Jack."

A small grin tipped his lips. "I know you do, and I love you too."

A commotion had her turning as a doctor in scrubs came towards her. "Are you the family of Victoria George?"

Astrid hadn't given Adeline's name and instead used the fake ID the paramedics had found in her pocket, and Astrid prayed it held up. The last thing she wanted was for whoever Adeline was hiding from to find her. "Yes. I'm her sister."

The doctor looked her up and down and then must have decided to believe her because he sat down beside her. "Your sister has suffered some very grave injuries indeed. We have repaired the bullet wound but it damaged her spleen, so we removed that. She has a broken jaw, three broken ribs, a fractured femur, and a dislocated shoulder. She'll require further surgeries, but the biggest worry is the bleed on her brain. We think a blunt instrument caused it and we've placed her in an induced coma to allow her time to heal."

Astrid pulled her lip between her teeth to try and control the sob forming and gripped Jack tighter. "Will she be okay?"

The doctor patted her shoulder gently. "We'll do our very best. We have a neurosurgeon on route who is the best in the world. Right now she's stable, and that's the best we can hope for."

Astrid heard every word he didn't say, and that was that Adeline probably wouldn't survive, but she was alive for now, and Astrid had to have hope. "Can I see her?"

"In a little while. The nurses need to get her settled in the ICU and then you can but only two at a time. She needs rest."

"Thank you." Taking a deep breath, she slowly blew it out, trying to hold on to her composure for a minute longer. "I need some air."

Jack nodded and steered her towards the doors that led out to the cool early afternoon air of Montreal in October. The sun shone brightly despite the cold and Astrid tipped her face to it, trying to absorb it and the hope it represented to her. Adeline had a battle on her hands, but she was a fighter, and so was Astrid. They'd get through this together.

CHAPTER TWENTY-ONE

JACK ROLLED over into the soft warmth of the woman who'd become his life and stroked his hand over her skin. It was three am, and he couldn't sleep. He'd fallen to sleep okay but had woken and wasn't sure why. He suspected it was because of the quiet, the lack of movement or action.

It had been six weeks since they'd flown home from Montreal after the tour was postponed, the Palace sighting the Prince Consort's mother being unwell for the reason which he'd learned was, in part, genuine. Adeline had been flown over as well and had been transferred to a private hospital in Hereford but was still in a coma, which he knew was churning Astrid up inside.

Her injuries were healing well, but the induced coma was now a real coma. That could happen, especially if it involved a head trauma. Doctor Savannah Sankey was a shock to him, not least because she was the same age as he was and was utterly brilliant. She'd won over Astrid's trust immediately. She was honest and open about Adeline's injuries and chances of recovery, and a full recovery was slim but not impossible. She was using new techniques to stimulate Adeline's brain.

The one holdout was Decker, who'd taken a dislike to the good doctor and looked for fault in everything she did, at least until this last week when he'd seemed to mellow a little. Jack wondered if it was because he was used to being the smartest person in a room, and the doctor challenged him. Decker needed that, someone to spar with on an intellectual level.

He felt Astrid shift, moving her ass back into his body as if seeking his touch even in her sleep and smiled. He'd never in his wildest dream thought this woman would be his soulmate, but she was. He had no doubt in his mind she was the one for him. She still drove him crazy with her untidiness and her perpetual need for new shoes, but he wouldn't change a thing about her.

He saw the loving, kind, funny woman under her snark now and struggled to understand how he'd missed it before. The passion between them was incendiary, and he wondered if it was that desire for her that had blinded him to who she was. Astrid brought chaos into his life and a primitive need in him to conquer her, and it had scared him but now he relished it.

The ringing of his phone had him tensing as he grabbed for it, seeing Will's name and knowing instinctively that it was bad news. Sitting up, he answered as Astrid rolled over, coming fully awake in seconds, her hand reaching for his.

"Will, what's wrong?"

"It's Mum, Jack. She's in the hospital. They think she's had a mini stroke."

Jack was already swinging his legs out of bed. "I'm on my way. What ward is she on?"

"She's still in accident and emergency while they do more tests."

"Okay, we'll be there soon."

He hung up feeling numb and looked at Astrid, who was already half-dressed and was ready to have his back no matter what.

"What is it, Jack?"

"That was Will. They think Mum had a mini stroke. She's at the hospital."

She came to him, her arms going around him and holding tight as he returned the hug, needing it more than he wanted to admit right now. Her scent, the familiar feel of her body against his, the touch of her hair all calmed the fear rattling around in his chest.

"Let's go find out what's happening."

He drove through the near-empty streets of the city he loved and pulled into the hospital car park in minutes. He saw Aubrey and Will's car parked and pulled in beside it. Whatever happened in there, they were coming out of this together.

Astrid took his hand and held it tight as they walked in and found Aubrey and Will waiting for them. Will looked pale and upset, but Aubrey held his hand tight, letting go only to hug Astrid. The two women had become closer than ever now that they were almost family, and they would be one day.

He had no doubt he'd make Astrid his wife and Will would do the same with Aubrey, if only they could catch a fucking break.

"How is she?"

"They've taken her for a scan to see if they can find what is going on."

Will sat heavily in the open waiting room. There was a drunk in the corner with a cut on his eye, a child crying with two obviously worried parents, and them.

Jack sat next to his brother, Astrid on his other side. "What happened?"

Will sighed. "She stayed overnight as she'd had dinner with us and was looking tired, so we asked her to stay. She woke Aubrey around three am to say she felt poorly and was slurring her speech. Then she passed out, so we called an ambulance."

"She's been looking tired lately. I told her to go to the doctor about it, but you know what Mum is like." Jack looked at the floor, feeling guilty for not spending as much time with his mum as he should.

Will smirked. "Stubborn!"

Jack pursed his lips. "Exactly."

Aubrey chuckled and shook her head. "Pot meet kettle."

Jack leaned around his brother to the woman who had long since become a sister to him. "Hey, I listen."

Aubrey raised one eyebrow. "Do you remember that, Astrid?" She looked around him now, and he leaned back so the girls could see each other.

"To be fair, he did listen when Valentina and Rafe told him to wear the arm guard when he was playing target for Ajax and Diablo."

"Good job, too or I'd only have one arm left. Those two are brutal."

"But so well trained. Val has them eating out of her hand."

"That's what I pay her for."

"Again, you listened when you were told you needed a dog unit. Good job, honey." Astrid looked at him with a wink, and he shook his head, pulling her closer to kiss her cheek.

"You two are nauseatingly sweet," Will groaned.

"Don't be jealous, bro. You have Aubrey."

"Yeah, but she's mean to me."

Aubrey glared at Will. "Um, excuse me?"

"You took my red lace candy away." Will pouted, and Jack laughed.

"Good for you, Aubrey." He held up his fist, and she bumped it with a smile. "You need to start eating like a grown up."

"Oh please, I've seen the sour Haribo's in your drawer at Eidolon."

"Boys, please. Let's agree you're both awesome and leave it at that, shall we? And for the record, if I didn't love you, William Granger, I wouldn't give a shit what you ate, so stop being a baby."

Jack smirked at his brother who glowered at him and mouthed. "See what you did?"

Jack kept quiet, not really wanting to cause a fight and just letting the banter take away the tension of not knowing what was happening with his mother. He knew Will was doing the same.

"How are Valentina and Rafe fitting into Eidolon?" Aubrey asked as she linked her fingers with Will's and his brother kissed her shoulder, the love between them deep and strong.

"Good, they've settled in well. It wasn't easy letting a new person into the team, let alone two, but I have good recommendations on both, and they work so well together. The dogs are amazing and a massive bonus for what we can achieve in such a short time."

"How many dogs do you have now?"

"Six. Ajax and Diablo are German Shepherds, Loki and Tiny are Bernese Mountain dogs. Buddy is a Cocker Spaniel, and Ziggy is a Malinois. I'm actually going to see if I can get Val and Rafe to teach the rest of the team how to work with the dogs too."

Aubrey grinned. "I'd be up for that as well if it's possible."

"Me too. I love dogs."

Jack squeezed Astrid's hand that hadn't left his. "You don't need an excuse to come and see me at work, firefly. We talked about this, and you're welcome to come to see me at any time."

Astrid swatted his arm. "Arrogant jerk and it wasn't an excuse. I'd love to work with them. Roz is thinking of getting some for Zenobi."

"Then I'll make it happen."

"I knew you would."

He felt his blood heat with desire for her when she smiled at him as if he could fix anything in the world with just his will alone. Astrid always believed in him and never failed to show it or have his back. Even when it was someone teasing as Aubrey had been, she'd still stood up for him and he loved her for it.

"Mr Granger?"

Jack and Will stood with the women they loved by their sides as a doctor called them through and asked them to take a seat in what was he knew a relative's room and, in his mind, it didn't bode well.

Astrid linked her fingers with his, and he was grateful to have her with him. "How is she?"

The doctor who was around his age clicked a button on a computer and faced the four of them. "She's suffered what we call a TIA or Transient Ischaemic Attack. It has resolved itself, but she will need to make some changes in her lifestyle and cut down on stress. We want to keep her for a few days just to run some more tests and make sure, but right now she's awake and asking to see you all, but it needs to be two at a time." The five of them stood as one. "She'll be moved onto a ward as soon as we can find her a bed."

"Thank you, doctor."

Jack thrust out his hand, and the doctor shook it with a nod. "You're welcome."

Astrid rubbed Jack's arm, offering comfort. "How about Aubrey and I go and get coffee, and you come to find us when you're ready?"

"That sounds good but stay inside the hospital. I don't want you wandering around outside in the middle of the night."

Astrid went on tiptoes and kissed him lightly, her lips soft against his. "Bossy."

"I love you."

"Now you're not playing fair."

Jack chuckled. "But it's true, I do."

"I know. Which is why I'll do as you ask—this time."

He gave her a wink and watched her and Aubrey walk down the corridor towards the all-night coffee shop.

He and Will walked through the double doors to the accident and emergency bays and looked around until his eyes found his mother. Relief came over his face when he saw her sitting up in bed, looking tired but alive. Anything else he could face but not losing his mother, not now, he wasn't ready.

Jack had always sought his father's approval, but it was his mum he turned to for love and guidance. She had been, and still was, the bedrock of the Granger family.

CHAPTER TWENTY-TWO

CAROLYN GRANGER WAS SITTING up in bed when they arrived at her bedside. Jack bent to kiss her soft cheek and she reached for his hand. "Hey, Mum, what you up to?"

"Scaring myself half to death apparently."

Jack and Will took seats on either side of her after Will had kissed her too. "You took ten years of my life as well."

Her cool blue eyes so much like his own met his, and she gripped her hand, the once strong woman looking older and more fragile than he'd ever seen her. "I'm sorry, son."

"Hey, don't be sorry, just concentrate on getting better. We need to help you out more."

Jack looked at Will, who nodded. "He's right, Mum. How about you come to stay with Brey and me for a while until you feel stronger?"

Carolyn looked at him with some of the fire in her eyes, and he saw a glimpse of the woman who'd chased him up the stairs with a wet dishrag when he gave her lip as a youngster. "I'm not an invalid, and I can take care of myself, thank you very much. I just need to make a few changes, that's all. This has been a long, arduous night, but I have some things I need to say to you both, and it is well over-due. I should have told you earlier, but a promise bound me. Now it's time for that secret to be shared."

Jack frowned and looked at Will, who shrugged his shoulders.

"What is going on, Mum?" Jack felt a knot form in his gut, a premonition of some revelation that couldn't be unsaid, and he wasn't sure he wanted to hear it.

"Back when Victoria was on the throne, she had a protective guard consisting of a small group of men who weren't part of the official royal guard. They were her own secret group who'd do her bidding and keep her safe from all who would harm her or her family."

"Like what we do?" Jack nodded his understanding, wondering where this history lesson was going.

"Yes, exactly like Eidolon. The first man who led her guard was called Alfred Granger, and he was your great, great, grandfather."

Jack felt his eyebrows hit his hairline and saw by his expression that Will was equally surprised by this news. "Wow."

"Indeed. Alfred was a great man who was loyal and honest, and he had three children, two sons and a daughter. The children would often play at the Palace, or so it is told, and his oldest daughter Eliza was good friends with the princess who would become Queen Louise. But Eliza would often take her younger brother Albie to play with them, as they were close in age. Evidently, Albie and Louise fell in love, and she had a child, a son, but they could never be together, and Eliza was sworn to secrecy. The child was given to Phillip, Eliza and Alfreds oldest brother to raise as his own with his wife barren it worked out perfectly and Albie was assured his child could keep the family name. Eliza and the Queen remained close until the day she died. Eliza documented all of it in her diaries which were unearthed long after her death."

Jack looked down at his feet as the implications of this story began to unfold in his mind and all of the ramifications that were coming to light.

"That child was your grandfather. The men of the Granger family continued to serve the reigning Monarchs of the family until your father. He got it in his head that he had a claim on the throne and was deemed by the Queen to be unfit to serve as part of her protection. So for the first time in a couple of generations a Granger was overlooked. As you can imagine that didn't sit well with him."

Jack stood, his brain struggling to quell the tension in his body that needed an outlet. He paced the small cubicle as Will sat back in his chair, looking as shocked as he was.

"So, let me get this straight. One, our family have always served as the Queen's guard, which is why she approached me." He ticked each point on his fingers. "Two, we have royal blood and are what? Distant cousins of the Queen? And three, Father has some asinine idea he should be King?"

"That about sums it up, dear, yes." His mum patted the bed, and he sat beside her taking her hand.

"Why now? Why keep this secret and tell us now? If I'd known before, I would've known what I was facing with Dad and his special brand of crazy."

"Because I've been released from my promise, and I fear your father is planning something that will end with my two most precious boys hurt. I know I didn't protect you before and I should have. I should've stopped his bullying and I didn't. For that I will be eternally sorry, but I do love you, and I'll do what I can to make it up to you."

"It's okay, Ma, we know you tried."

Jack glanced at Will, who looked stunned and hurt, the pain that had been caused by their father so much worse than what he'd had. Frederick had done nothing but show Will contempt from the beginning.

Jack gripped his brother's shoulder in support. "Why was he harder on Will than me?"

"Frederick wasn't always the man he is today. He was kind and gentle, but he was the product of a strict father who wanted him to be the best and always found fault. When the Queen passed over him, it almost killed him. Will was born around the same time, and I think that coupled with the fact he couldn't control his youngest child, he lashed out. I should have left him then, but I didn't, and I'm sorry."

"It's okay. I didn't need Dad. I had Jack and you."

"It is not okay, but I love you for saying that, baby boy."

Jack chuckled at his mother's name for Will. He was so far from that scrawny child now. He was a man, a protector, an inventor, and could buy and sell this country he loved over and over so great was his wealth, which he barely touched.

"Why does Dad want Eidolon destroyed? Is it pure jealousy?"

Carolyn looked at him then. "He wants the throne, and in his head, if he can take down the Queen, he can make that play. He has reams and reams of paperwork pertaining to his lineage. Plus, I think there's a little revenge for the Queen passing him over and a lot of hurt pride."

"Jesus, what kind of father tries to ruin his own sons for pride and power and some title?"

Will looked at him with sad eyes. "A shit one."

"So eloquent, William, no wonder Aubrey loves you."

Will smiled as he gave him the middle finger.

Jack saw his mother yawn, and he and Will stood. "We should let you get some rest. Two things before we go, though."

"Yes, love?"

"How do you know all this? And who was the promise to?"

His mother smiled sadly. "Your father told me when we first married, and the rest came over time as he'd rant and rave about it. I didn't know he was targeting Eidolon, or I would've told you sooner."

"I know, Ma. We kept it from you on purpose. We didn't want you dragged into this shit with us."

"Language, Jack."

"Sorry, this nightmare."

"Well, I am now, and I support my sons completely. If I hear from Frederick, I'll let you know, but I doubt I will now." He could hear the slight melancholy in her voice as if she remembered the past and better times.

"Who was the promise to?"

Carolyn smiled wide. "My good friend Lydia."

Jack felt his jaw go slack in shock, sure he must be hearing his mother wrong. "Not *the* Lydia, the Queen?"

"Yes, exactly. Who do you think got on a train to London to warn her of your father's intentions all those years ago?"

"Holy crap. Go, Mum."

"I may have loved him, but I wasn't blind to the threat he posed to the Queen, and I didn't want that for my sons. Unfortunately, I may have made it worse for them."

Jack leaned down, his hand on his mother's head and kissed her forehead. "Love you, Mum. Get some rest and Astrid and I will be in to see you tomorrow."

"I do love that girl, and she suits you so well."

Jack smiled, unable to help it when he thought of Astrid. "Yeah, she does."

Jack moved back so Will could say goodbye, and he and his brother walked out of the department to find Astrid and Aubrey in silence.

Halfway down the corridor, he angled his body towards Jack. "Can you believe all that?"

He shook his head. "I believe it because Mum wouldn't lie to us about something like that, but I can't wrap my head around it at all, not in the fucking least."

"Me neither."

"It explains a lot, though. Like how easily I got the contract for Eidolon and why I was the one they contacted."

"Yeah, it also explains the email I got asking me to set up the funds and company."

Jack stopped, and Will turned back to him. "They emailed and asked you to set up Eidolon? I thought it was your idea."

"Well, it was, but I received an email suggesting I should use the funds and I should make use of your talent. The natural thought process led me to a Black Ops team."

"Was it from Fitz?"

Will nodded. "I traced it back to him, yes."

Jack resumed walking, wanting to get to Astrid now and tell her everything. "That sneaky fucker."

"Yeah, but it worked out. Eidolon is a force to be reckoned with now because of you, Jack."

"I appreciate you saying that, brother, but without your funds, it wouldn't be what it is today."

"We make a good team, don't we?"

Jack slung his arm over his brother's shoulders. "We sure do."

Will grinned. "Astrid has changed you, Jack."

"For the better?"

"Not better or worse, she's just shown you it's okay to let go sometimes, to show people how you feel."

"It's hard to undo a lifetime of conditioning, but I'm trying."

"You've always been a good man, Jack. Who else spends thousands of pounds on play equipment so his admin manager can bring her daughter to work?"

"Hey, without Autumn I'd be lost. That's just good business sense and she's worth every penny."

"Whatever, bro."

"What do you think the girls will make of this?"

"Not sure, but there's Aubrey now. Let's find out."

"Hey, Brey. Where's Astrid?"

Her panicked look suddenly registered on Jack's face, and his chest tightened with anxiety.

"I don't know. She went to the toilet fifteen minutes ago and never came back. I checked everywhere, and I can't find her."

Jack's whole world seemed to fade to nothing except the urgent need to get Astrid back to him where she belonged, and he didn't care what or who he had to kill to make that happen.

His phone rang, and he saw it was Alex. "Alex."

"Jack, police just found a bomb outside the Palace gates. We need to go."

He knew this was his father. Divide and conquer was his aim and by attacking the Palace he knew Jack would send his team to protect the Queen while holding Astrid over Jack's head. "I can't. My father has Astrid."

"Fuck." Alex sounded torn.

Divide and conquer, except his father hadn't bargained on his secret weapon.

"Take the team and Fortis to the Palace. I need to find Astrid."

"Jack, who's going to help you?"

"I have Zenobi and my family."

Jack hung up safe in the knowledge that Alex could handle things and called the one woman he'd vowed never to ask for help.

"Roz, I need your help."

CHAPTER TWENTY-THREE

"Jack is going to kill you when he finds out you've taken me." Astrid glared at the man she'd only seen in pictures and hated that she saw any of Jack in his handsome face, but the two men looked alike. It was inside where they were like night and day. Jack was a protector, a hero, and a loyal friend; his father was nothing but a roach.

He flicked his wrist in an off-hand manner that made Astrid want to break his face. "My sons will never kill me. Jack is too soft to kill the man who gave him life and William is nothing more than a nuisance."

"Yeah, well I won't have any such hesitation, asshole." She wriggled her cuffed wrists against the pipe in the cellar of a large old house she knew too well. It was the cellar of Jack's mother's home.

Frederick laughed and it made her itch to throat punch the fucker who'd tried to ruin the man she loved.

"You're a delight. I can see why Jack is having fun with you. Of course, you'll not do for the long term. With a family such as ours, breeding is important, and we can't have you polluting the bloodline."

Astrid twisted to get more comfortable on the cold floor which only contained an old set of garden furniture and two dog beds, nothing she could use, at least that she could see. "What the hell are you talking about, old man? Bloodline? Have you finally lost your mind and joined the cuckoo clan?"

She probably shouldn't bait him, but she was angry with herself that he'd got the jump on her at the hospital and furious that Jack would now be going out of his mind with worry and blaming himself.

"I wouldn't expect you to understand, a mere American with no class or breeding. Jack is destined for greatness. When I take the throne with him at my side, we'll rule this great land and make it a force to be feared again."

Astrid snorted as Frederick crouched down, not a crease on his impeccably cut suit. "Fred, you're whacked if you believe Jack will do anything with you. He hates your guts."

"Because he doesn't have the facts and you're going to help me with that. Jack seems to have affection for you so he will come, and I'll explain it all."

"Jack isn't a fool. He won't fall into a trap. He has his entire team at his back, even though you tried to break them."

"Ah, silly girl, do you think I would be so foolish? Eidolon will soon be on their way to London to save the Queen from the bombs I had planted, leaving Jack here alone to save the girl he thinks he loves."

Jack did love her. She'd had a man who'd said it and didn't mean it, and she knew the difference. Jack not only said it, he showed it every way—from the soft look he saved just for her that said she was his entire world, to the way he let her leave her stuff all over his home, even though mess drove him nuts, and the fact he brought her coffee in bed before he left for work every morning. All those things showed her how much he loved her, and she loved him with a fierceness she'd never experienced before.

She'd heard people say they would die for those they loved and never got it until him. Astrid would walk through fire for him, would happily take a bullet to save his life, and she was damned if she'd let this man harm him.

"You're wrong, he does love me, and Jack will find a way. He always does, because he's a hero, not a traitor like you."

The blow to her face was sharp and painful, her head hitting the wall behind her as Frederick backhanded her. She tasted blood on her tongue and her vision blurred, but she fought it, not allowing him to see her pain. She'd suffered far worse being done to her and survived.

"You will call Jack and tell him to wait for my call tomorrow at noon. If you don't, then I'm afraid your sister will be handed over to the men hunting her."

Astrid felt her blood run cold. It was the one threat that could make her rigid spine crumble. Eidolon and Zenobi were protecting her sister, and Lopez was a near-permanent fixture at the private hospital where she was still in a coma but recovering.

"You're bluffing."

"Am I? Your sister Adeline is currently in Beaverbrook Private Hospital under constant guard, but do you want to take the risk that with my son's team gone, she'll be safe?"

Astrid felt her mouth water like she was going to be sick and swallowed over and over to keep the bile at bay. "Did you send Ravelino after me?"

Frederick stood and paced to the other side of the room before turning with a smug look on his face. "I did. You see, when I saw the way my Jack looked at you, I knew there was something I could use. So, I looked into you and found some fascinating facts. You're former CIA and escaped from Ravelino when they blew your cover. I figured there was unfinished business there and that I could use them. I unleashed the dogs if you will. They did the dirty work, although I had assumed they would be better than they were and actually capture or at least kill you."

He walked back towards her, and she was sure she could see her face in his highly polished shoes.

"I didn't count on my son's team being so good, and I should have. That was my mistake."

Astrid could hear the note of pride in Fredericks's voice and was shocked by how crazy he sounded. She knew how Jack had spent his life looking for his father's pride and now for her to hear it, after everything he'd put Jack through made her feel sick. "You're a piece of shit, you know that, Fred?"

"Make the call." He pushed a phone towards her, his face florid with anger, his eyebrow ticking, showing he wasn't as calm as he wanted her to think he was.

"Uncuff me, asshole, so I can dial."

"No, give me the number and I'll dial it."

Astrid rolled her eyes and gave him the number, trying to figure out how she could send Jack a clue.

Barking from upstairs caught her attention and then she knew. The dogs were upstairs and would need feeding with Carolyn in the hospital. She just needed him to know where she was, but he'd come now, and she needed to end this herself before Jack had to. He would kill his father to protect her; she knew it in her heart, but she also knew it would break something inside him to do it, and she couldn't live with that on her conscience. She'd find a way to take Frederick down before he ever got the chance to put Jack in that position.

"You need to wait until the dogs have stopped barking or Jack will hear them." She hated helping this man in any way, but it was for the greater good.

"Ah, so not so stupid after all."

Frederick disappeared for a few minutes, as he went upstairs, and she could hear him walking around, probably giving the dogs those chews they loved to shut them up. Her mind went to Jack. She'd spent so long wanting him that she'd been afraid he'd break her heart by the time she had him, and she couldn't have been further from the truth.

He made her feel strong, nurtured the side she showed the world which was full of sass and fire but fed and nourished the side she kept for him, which was soft and vulnerable. He'd shown her what it felt like to be loved and to love with no expectations or limits, and she wasn't giving him up now or ever—not without a fight.

Footsteps on the old, wooden steps made her look up as Frederick came back and held out the ringing phone.

"Hello?" He sounded cautious and wary, and she prayed his mother was okay.

"Jack."

"Astrid, oh thank God. Are you okay? Has he hurt you?"

"I'm fine. Look, you need to wait for a call from your father at noon tomorrow. He'll give you instructions."

"Is he there?"

"Yes."

"Put him on the line."

She heard the steel in her man's voice and knew Frederick had picked a fight he couldn't win. "He wants to speak with you."

Frederick smiled and put the phone to his ear. "My boy, I apologise for the way this is playing out."

Astrid saw Frederick go still, his smug smile falling, his eyes pulling together in a frown. "When you hear what I have to say, I assure you, you'll think differently, my son."

His eyes flashed to her, and he looked angry again, the pulse in his temple throbbing. "Your mother needs to keep her mouth shut and know her place, then maybe I wouldn't have had to poison her to shut her up."

Astrid heard the roar that came down the line—not the words, just the fury. Frederick had gone after the two things Jack loved the most, her and his mother, and now he'd see the beast he'd awoken.

CHAPTER TWENTY-FOUR

A ROAR RIPPED from Jack as he hurled his phone across the room, watching with red tinging his vision as it smashed into pieces. His breathing was hard as he paced the room in an effort to control the rage pouring through his blood. Never in his life had he wanted to kill his father, not even after everything he'd done to him and Will—until now. Now Jack wasn't sure he'd even be able to stop himself if he wanted to.

His father had threatened and hurt the two women he loved most in the world and he'd pay for that. He opened his eyes and looked at Will, who was watching him silently. "He's been poisoning her."

Will sat forward, his body tense as he felt the strain of the last twenty-four hours too. "Sorry, what?"

"Mum. He said she should've kept her mouth shut and he wouldn't have had to poison her."

The chair hit the floor as Will jumped up. "That bastard."

"We should let the hospital know so they can run her blood and find out what it is and if it has any lasting effects. Then find out how so we can stop it." Jack nodded at Aubrey, who hadn't left them since his father had taken Astrid. Jack knew she was blaming herself, but he didn't. She would've likely ended up dead if she'd tried to stop him, and he couldn't live with that. "Can you handle that?"

"Yes, of course." Aubrey stood, dropped a kiss on Will and went to use Alex's office.

"Any word from Alex?"

Jack folded his arms over his chest and leaned against his desk, legs spread. "Yes, he says they've found four devices around the perimeter and that they're sweeping the entire Palace, but they've secured the Queen in an unknown location."

"Unknown to you?"

"Yes, I don't want to be compromised in any way, so the less I know, the better."

"You think he'll use Astrid to try and get the location from you?"

Jack snorted. "I know he will."

An alarm from the gatehouse had him looking at the monitor to see Roz with four of her girls. He pressed the button to let them in and moved to the door as Will followed.

"Never thought I'd see the day you and Roz worked together."

"Me neither, but I'd work with Satan himself if it meant getting Astrid back safe."

"You love her a lot."

Jack glanced at his brother and nodded. "More than I ever thought possible. I can't lose her."

Will squeezed his shoulder. "We won't, Jack. She's sharp. She'll stay alert until we can find her."

Jack shook his head. "I don't think she wants me to find her. She could've given me any number of clues and didn't. I think she plans to handle this on her own so I don't have to."

The fear of that realisation hit him in his heart, and he had to force himself to stay focused through it, or he'd make a mistake.

"She's trying to protect you."

"I don't want her protection, dammit. I want her safe. It's my job to protect her, not the other way around."

"I'm sorry to say, brother, you didn't fall in love with a meek woman who's willing to sit back and be saved. The women we love are warriors in their own right and they love us enough to want to protect us too. We have to accept that because it's part of the reason we love them."

"I'm not sure if I can."

"You already made a choice, Jack. Now you have to have the conviction to stand by it."

"So, what? I just sit back and let her take risks?"

"No, of course not. We go find that asshole, kick his ass, and save the girl, but we don't underestimate Astrid either."

Jack nodded, understanding his brother's words, having seen it time and again with his men, but he'd not fully understood the terror they felt until now.

The door opened and Roz walked in, looking around and taking note of everything. "Jack."

"Roz. Thank you for coming."

Bebe, Laverne, Pax, and a heavily pregnant Evelyn were with her.

"Evelyn, you do realise Alex would lose his mind if he found out you were here?"

Evelyn patted Jack's chest. "Chill, big guy. I'm here for support only, as is Pax."

"Thank God."

"Show me to the war room."

Jack started walking. "War room?"

"That's what you military guys call it, isn't it?"

Jack shook his head. "If by war room you mean the operations room, then no, we call it the operations room."

Roz waved her hand around. "Whatever. Have you heard from Frederick?"

"Yes, Astrid called and said he's going to call me at noon tomorrow and to wait to hear from him."

"Did she sound pissed?"

"Yeah, she did."

"Good. She never should have allowed him to get the drop on her like that. I trained her better."

Jack tried to bite his tongue, not wanting to get into it with Roz when he needed her help, but he was damned if he was going to stand by and let Roz get away with her words. "Listen, if you're going to bad mouth her, you can leave. That is the woman I love, and nobody gets to say anything negative about her in front of me."

"As it should be. Now, shall we get to it?"

Jack took his place behind the wide desk that held all the equipment while Roz and the others spread out. Will took his place at the computers and began bringing up images from around the hospital.

"We know he got her away at gunpoint, but she was walking in this image and got into the car on her own accord. We assume he threatened my mother or one of us, so she went willingly. He confessed to poisoning my mum, which means he wanted us at the hospital and we played into his hands without knowing it."

Roz raised her perfectly arched brow. "Wow, and I thought my father was an asshole."

"The CCTV picks them up heading out of town. Once they hit the countryside we lost track, so we don't know where he took her, but my guess is somewhere close. He's a creature of habit and will work with what he knows best."

Evelyn leaned back in her chair, her huge bump making the naturally graceful woman look awkward. "You couldn't trace the call?"

"No."

"Hmm, and is there anything out that way that you know of? A house or residence of any kind?" Pax crossed her legs as she spoke, looking a little paler than usual from her pregnancy and Jack was proud these women had stepped up for Astrid.

"Not that we know of and believe me, we've been looking."

"He has to be somewhere though, and close if he's been making visits to your mother's home undetected." Roz rolled her throwing stars through her knuckles as she spoke.

"I know."

"Is he alone?"

"We believe so. He seems to have sent all the men he has working for him to London. My guess is he thinks he can talk me around and doesn't need force, especially when he has Astrid."

"So, he's an idiot who underestimates his sons a lot. Got it."

Jack had no intention of telling Roz the extent of his father's crazy plan, or at least the story behind it, but they needed to know some of it. "He wants to overthrow the crown and plans to use me to do it."

"Then we need to find him so you can get some payback before our girl Astrid kills him."

Jack eyed Roz, hands on his hips. "My girl. Astrid is mine, and I'll protect her."

Roz stood and walked to him slowly. "She's Zenobi."

Jack and Roz were almost nose to nose. "She's mine. I love her."

"But you don't own her."

"No, she owns me. Completely and totally."

Jack saw a grin quirk Roz's lips as she nodded. "Fair enough."

The eight of them spent the next three hours working through the CCTV they had and any knowledge they had of Frederick, which was less than they needed.

"I've got it," Will shouted and Jack ran to the computer and looked over his shoulder.

"Wait, that's Mum's place."

Will looked up, his eyes bright with discovery despite the exhaustion. "I know, but I isolated all the sounds and kept picking up the sound of school kids. You know the noise kids make when they gather in the mornings."

"Yeah, I do. I hear it every damn morning." Jack's mind was already on the move. "So, you think he has Astrid there?"

"No, I know. Look!"

Will sped up the images and saw a different car than the one Frederick had first used pull up outside his mother's home and pull into the garage.

"So, no visual, but the odds are it's Frederick and Astrid."

"Yes."

Roz stood. "Let's go."

"Wait, we should make a plan."

Roz sighed but relented. "Fine, let's plan."

Over the last few hours she seemed to have ceded control of the operation to him, and he had a feeling it was because he'd faced her down over how she spoke about Astrid. It had been an asinine test on reflection, and he'd passed. Women, he was realising, thought differently to men, but it was a good thing. The ideas they had were more outside the box, more prone to emotion, but that was a good thing too.

"I should go in first. It's me he wants anyway. You can provide back-up, so he doesn't get away and just in case he has any surprises planned."

Will shook his head. "That's a bad plan. He could kill you."

Jack shook his head. "No, I don't think he will. He wants me to help him, so he needs me alive."

Will sighed. "I don't like it."

"Noted, brother, but may I remind you that you stole a plane and flew to the other side of the world to protect Aubrey."

"Fine, but I'm on comms."

"Fine by me."

Jack spent the next hour talking through the property's layout with Roz, Bebe, Laverne, and Aubrey who had insisted on coming even when Will hit the roof. They had then revised the plan so Will would go with them too. Jack understood it now because he felt the same.

"Ready?"

"Let's go get your girl back before she does something stupid."

Roz pushed past him at the exit, always needing the last word but he'd take that. Without Zenobi, this would be much harder.

· · ·

THE HOUSE WAS dark when they arrived, hiking in from the back roads and over the fields rather than coming in directly. His mother's home, the house he'd grown up in, was only two roads over from his own place, and Will had picked up on the same school kids he heard every morning.

The house was a four-storey Victorian home on a quiet side road with a large garden overlooking the black mountains. Jack held up a fist as they approached, and everyone stopped moving. Two armed guards were stationed at the back door.

Lucy, a colleague and friend from Fortis, who'd not gone to London and was also ex-Zenobi, had stepped up to run comms for them.

"We have two armed guards at the back. Do you see any more inside?"

"*I have four heat signatures inside on the ground floor and one in the basement.*"

Jack took a deep breath. She was alive. "Aubrey, this is a shoot to kill mission, so if you want to walk away, I'll understand. You're an officer of the law, after all."

"Fuck that. I'm family, and he messed with that."

Jack smiled; this was why he loved his sister-in-law.

"Roz, I need you, Bebe, and Laverne to take out the guards at the front and hold the position, in case he has back-up stationed close by. Aubrey, Will, and I will secure the men at the back and inside. I'll then head downstairs, which is where my father will run to when he hears us."

"*Copy that.*"

Jack crept forward, fighting his instincts to rush to Astrid instead of using his training to make sure this was done correctly. His father was a master strategist and would expect Jack to come for him, so he needed to be creative.

"Execute, execute, execute."

At his words they all moved. He took out the first guard as Aubrey downed the second, both dead from kill shots. Jack heard Roz and the girls breach the front and take down the man stationed just inside, as he came through from the back and took out the two remaining men. That meant his father was in the basement with Astrid.

"Secure the house. I'm going down."

Jack made sure his weapon was secure at his back, knowing his father would take the other from him and probably that one too but hopefully not the knife in his boot.

The steps creaked as he descended and he got his first look at Astrid in nine hours. She looked tired but pissed, a cut on her lip made his jaw twitch in anger but he remained outwardly calm as he focused on the man who'd made this all happen.

He looked as polished as always, his three-piece suit buttoned, hair combed, and shoes polished to a military shine. Yet Jack knew he was a fraud and a traitor, not only to his country but to his family.

He levelled his weapon on his father. "Give me one good reason why I shouldn't kill you where you stand."

"I can give you two. Firstly, you'll want to hear what I have to say, and secondly, because if you do, her sister dies."

Jack's eyes flashed to Astrid who nodded sadly, and he knew that was why she hadn't made a move yet, but he could see by the fact her bindings were almost cut through that she was about to. "Fine, say your piece."

"Come along, Jack. Put the weapon down. I don't want to have to kill Adeline, but I will." Jack lowered his weapon to the ground and moved until he was in front of Astrid. If Frederick wanted her, he had to go through him.

"Now that's better. Your mother has said some things she shouldn't have, so let me have my say."

"Jack, I have people on their way to Beaverbrook hospital to secure Adeline as we speak."

Jack could hear Lucy talking over the comms and knew she'd have his back. He just needed to keep Frederick busy until Adeline was secure. "Fine, say your piece."

"Your mother was a good woman, but she lost her direction. I blame myself for being away so much and not being there to guide her."

Jack clenched his fists. "Enough, get on with it."

"The Queen should not be on the throne. Her line is a lie. My grandfather was the rightful heir. He may have been illegitimate, but he was the first-born child of the woman who would be Queen. Therefore, when she died, it should have come to us."

"That's not how it works and you know it. He wasn't recognised by the crown and from my understanding, he had a good life with wealth and privilege, along with a seat at the Queen's side regardless, because of the Guard."

"We should be recognised. It is our right." Frederick was red in the face, a vein in the centre of his forehead pulsing with it as he made the statement.

"So, what's your plan? Kill the Queen, overthrow the Monarchy, and claim the power for yourself?"

"For us, son. This is for you. One day you'll have children and understand the sacrifices we parents make to ensure your futures."

"Bullshit, this is for you. All you ever did was treat Will like shit. You had him locked up to cover for your crimes for fuck's sake. Who does that to their own son?"

"Will was weak, rebellious. He never learned when to shut up and toe the line. Not like you. You were an exemplary soldier, brave and loyal. Will would have ruined that. An endeavour like this requires money and I could get that if I helped out men like al-Sabir."

"Will is everything you're not. Good, kind, loyal, and so damn clever he borders on genius and you're too stupid to see it. He's made more money than you could spend in ten lifetimes, and still, he's humble and ready to put himself on the line for the good of others. You just want to lie and deceive and climb some imaginary ladder. He's a hundred times the man you are."

"You don't mean that."

"Adeline is secure. He was bluffing."

It was time to wrap this up.

"I do mean it. You're dead to me. I'll never help you."

"Then her sister dies." His father pulled a gun and moved so it was pointing at Astrid.

Jack moved with him, grabbing the weapon from his back, and holding it steady on his father. He didn't want to kill him, but he'd protect his firefly. "Her sister is secure. You were bluffing."

"Motherfucker." Astrid spat from behind him, and in any other situation he'd find it amusing.

He kept his eyes on Frederick. "Get up, firefly."

"Bossy."

Jack glanced down at Astrid for a split second. "Seriously? Can we do this later?"

"Fine."

He felt her grab his leg and take the knife from his boot before she stood.

"It's over, Frederick."

"No, it will never be over, and if I go down, so do you. I did all my transactions in your name."

Jack shook his head, shocked at the depths he'd go to. "No, I won't because Will fixed that. You have two options now, die or surrender."

"You won't kill me."

"I don't want to, but I will, to stop you."

Jack felt the back of his neck tingle and moved to look behind him. A gun went off and he felt pain explode in his chest followed by the sight of his father falling to the ground, dead from a single shot to the head.

CHAPTER TWENTY-FIVE

ASTRID STEPPED into Jack's office at Eidolon after her shower and locked the door. He was sitting at his desk, looking no worse for wear after being shot in the chest by his asshole of a father who was now deceased.

Her heart beat double time thinking of what might have been if he hadn't been wearing one of the bulletproof vests Will had designed. It was simple for her—he'd hurt those she loved and deserved to die, but she knew for Jack and Will it was more complex. He'd given them life, and now he was dead.

Bás appearing at the eleventh hour and somehow bypassing everyone upstairs to get to the cellar and kill Frederick was somewhat of a shock. Bás shooting and killing Frederick as the man pulled the trigger on his own son was a relief to her though. Killing his dad would have taken something from Jack. Left a hole that nothing could heal and would've changed the man she loved inside. It was a debt she'd gladly owe Bás, although when she'd thanked him, he'd brushed it off as nothing. The man was an enigma, but she didn't care about him right now. Her focus was Jack and what he needed.

"You doing okay?"

Jack twisted his chair to face her as she moved around the desk to him. He held his arms out to her as his eyes took her in from head to foot like a starving man. "I'm fine now you're here."

Astrid sat on his lap, looping her arms around his neck, the feel of his hard, firm body beneath her making arousal flood through her with needy desperation. His scent, so familiar now,6 never failed to set her alight with need but more than that, he smelled like home to her.

"I love you, Jack." Her hand ran over his face, the stubble tickling her palm as he held her tight to him as if afraid to let go. This big alpha protector was shaken by what had happened, and she wanted to soothe him.

"I love you too, more than you'll ever know, and I'm so sorry."

Her finger found his lips, stopping the apology that wasn't his to give. "No, this isn't yours to make. Frederick alone did this, and he's dead now and can't hurt you anymore."

"Maybe not, but I do regret that Frederick took you."

"I know, but none of this is on you. You're everything he wasn't. I used to think you were stuffy, but you're not. You're solid and dependable, kind, and sexy as sin."

"Oh yeah?"

She grazed her lips over his ear, her hand sliding the zip of his fly down so she could feel the hard length of him in her hand. His breath hissed out as she grasped his erection, sweeping her hand over the pre-cum gathered at the tip.

Jack cupped her chin, forcing her eyes to him. "I need to feel you, firefly."

"Then take me, Jack."

He stood with her in his arms and placed her ass on the edge of his desk. Sweeping his hand wide, paperwork and stationery fell to the floor as he cleared his desk for her. His hand in the centre of her chest, he pushed until she was half lying on his desk, her feet dangling to the floor as he stepped between her legs. He looked magnificent, all dark and brooding but with the soft light of love on his face for her—only ever her.

His eyes devoured her, the blue her favourite storm, his hands stroked over her skin as he drew her sweats—the only thing she could find in his locker to wear—down her legs, taking her panties with them. His palm pressed to her mound, the heel of it applying delicious pressure to her clit.

She moaned as she reached for his cock, stroking over him as he positioned himself at her entrance. This wasn't about making love, this was about affirming life and their connection. Jack swept his cock through the wetness of her desire as he reached behind his nape with one hand and drew his shirt over his head, revealing the bruise from the bullet hitting the vest and the defined muscles which made her so tongue-tied.

"Lose the shirt, firefly."

She had no argument when he went all alpha on her; it turned her on like nothing else. Shucking her shirt, she saw pleasure tinge his cheeks when he saw she was braless.

He gripped her hips and pushed into her, hard and fast, her body instantly adjusting to his size as she cried out in pleasure. The feeling of being full as she pulsed around his dick made her whimper. He didn't stop to let her adjust but began to fuck her hard and fast, his face a mask of brutal strength and beauty.

"Promise you'll never leave me."

His words affected her, making her feel wanted, needed. "Yes."

"Say it. Say the words."

"I'll never leave you, Jack. I'm yours."

She felt him shudder as he began to move faster, his thumb on her clit, the desk moving with each thrust.

"And I'm yours, firefly, for as long as you want me or until the day I die."

Her heart and body felt full of love for this man, and she knew she'd never stop loving him. He was her soulmate, and she was his. "Never. I'll never not want you, Jack."

"My soulmate, my heart."

Her body pulsed and her climax hit, almost drowning out the beauty of his words, but he whispered them against her neck as he let his climax take him and collapsed against her body, her arms holding him tight against her.

"I love you, firefly. I don't deserve you, and I certainly don't know what you see in me when you're such rare beauty both inside and out, but I'll never stop loving you or thanking the universe that I have you."

"Jack, you're so..."

His finger covered her lips. "Don't ruin it, firefly."

Astrid laughed, feeling free for the first time in a decade. She still had battles to fight, but she'd do them with this man by her side.

———

IT FELT strange to be back at the Palace. Her perspective of it had changed now she knew her man had links to this place and any children they might have would too. They hadn't discussed kids, but she knew she wanted them with Jack and that he'd make a wonderful father.

Fitz greeted her with a warm smile. "Good to see you, Astrid, Jack."

Jack and Fitz shook hands, and Astrid smiled. "Hi, Fitz. Are you well?"

"Yes, perfectly thank you, and it's good to see you looking the same after your ordeal."

Astrid waved it off. That was hardly even a blip and had it been anyone else, she wouldn't have thought twice about escaping and killing him. "It was nothing."

Fitz leaned into Jack as they waited for the Queen to allow them entrance. "You have your hands full with this one."

Jack looked at her with a smirk. "I wouldn't have it any other way." He winked, and her blood pressure soared. Trust Jack to get her worked up right before an important visit with the Monarch.

A bell rang, and Fitz nodded and went ahead of them.

Astrid poked him in his hard abs. "You cannot flirt with me like that before we see the head of state."

Jack caught her finger and pulled her close. "I can and I will." His lips found hers in a short but hot kiss, stealing her breath before he released her and winked again.

Astrid scowled but honestly, she didn't care. She'd spent a lifetime wanting a man like Jack to look at her precisely as he was, and she'd never get angry at him for loving her or wanting her.

"She will see you now."

Astrid and Jack stepped into the royal parlour and saw Queen Lydia looking as perfect as ever. Astrid dropped into a curtsey as Jack gave a short bow.

"It is so good to see you looking so well."

"Thank you, ma'am."

"Please sit." Lydia motioned to the two wing back seats, and Astrid waited for the Queen to sit before she and Jack followed suit.

She folded her hands over her lap and regarded him. "How are you, Jack?"

He was wearing a navy suit today and looked every bit the secret agent. "Relieved it is all over, ma'am."

"Yes, I'm sure you are, but it is still sad to lose a parent, and I know these were difficult circumstances at best."

"It is hard to put into words without sounding callous, ma'am. I have wonderful people around me, so I feel exceedingly lucky." He glanced at her, and she smiled.

"You certainly do. How is your mother?"

"She is fine. He was leaking the poison into the water where she gets her supply. It's now clean, and she should have no lasting effects from it."

"Good, I'm glad to hear that. Now, I know Carolyn told you everything, but do you have any questions for me?"

"I've thought about this a lot, and I honestly don't. I may in the future but right now, I have none. This changes nothing for me. I am who I am, and I'm where I'm meant to be. The throne is in the best hands it could be in, and I'm honoured just to share any blood with you."

"That is very gracious, Jack. You're an honourable man and one I consider a close friend of the family. I would greatly like it if you will stay on in your position. There is nobody I feel safer entrusting my safety to than you and your team."

"It is my honour, ma'am. And if one day our children wish to know about their history?"

Astrid felt butterflies in her tummy as he looked at her.

"Then, when the time is right, you can handle that, and there will always be a position for a person such as yourself on my staff if they wish it."

"Thank you, ma'am. I do have one question actually."

Lydia cocked her head. "Yes."

"Bás. Who does he really work for?"

"Ah, that was my husband's doing. You see, when Frederick began to make waves, it became clear we needed someone he'd never know about on the inside, so to speak. My husband hired Bás to ensure Frederick was in check and to keep you safe. I know that there were times when he perhaps should've stepped in and revealed himself. Instead, we let things happen, which on reflection we shouldn't have. But Bás had to ensure his cover, and in the end, it paid off."

"What will happen now? As you know, I'm setting up a second team which is even more secret than Eidolon, and I was hoping Bás would lead it."

Jack had told Astrid all about Shadow Elite and the role they would play, and she'd even recommended one or two people she thought might be a good fit for the team which he'd taken on board.

There were no secrets between them, but it did mean there were secrets between her and Roz now, which was why she'd resigned from Zenobi. She didn't feel it was fair to split her loyalties when she knew deep down Jack would always come first. She was now free to care for her sister if she ever came out of the coma and would help with the Queen's protection, which she enjoyed. Roz hadn't been happy, but she'd understood and told her she was always welcome back in the future if she changed her mind.

Astrid would miss working with them. They were a strong group of women who'd saved her in more ways than she'd ever be able to thank them for, but she also knew she had friends for life who would die for her and her them. That made her lucky in so many ways. Plus, she was now officially a WAG—a wife or girlfriend—of one of the Eidolon men according to Evelyn.

"He is free to do as he wishes. He has been released from his duty now the threat is gone."

"Thank you, ma'am."

"I do hope I'll get an invitation to the wedding when you two tie the knot." The Queen smiled wide, and Astrid blushed as Jack grabbed her hand with a grin.

"I haven't asked her yet, Your Majesty, but when I do, you'll be at the top of the list."

"Oh, good. I do love a wedding. You will stay for lunch?"

"We'd love to."

Jack answered for them, and Astrid was happy to stay too. She'd missed Lydia and would always be there any time she needed her.

EPILOGUE

Jack had never been so nervous in his life. He'd rather face down a room full of insurgents with a pair of knitting needles than this, but he was also excited. Valentine's Day had seemed like a long time away when he'd set this plan into action, but it had come around quicker than he'd realised. He guessed that's what happened when you were truly happy, and after so many years the heavy load on his shoulders was lifted.

Astrid was with her sister who was still in a coma. Each day she stayed that way a little more hope that she'd ever come out of it died. His heart ached for the woman he loved who'd gotten her sister back only to have her snatched away. He'd agreed when she'd decided not to tell her parents anything. Why give them hope when there may not be any.

Jack checked again to make sure he had everything he needed and waited. He didn't have to wait long before he heard the keys in the lock. Astrid had moved in with him just after Christmas, and he'd never been happier in his life. She was everything to him. Just the thought of her made him smile and a day away from her felt like a year he missed her so much.

He now knew how his men felt about the women they loved. Alex was now a father to a daughter named Liliana, but they called her Lily for short, and Mitch's wife Autumn had given birth to a son they'd named Devon.

Waggs and Willow had gotten engaged just before Christmas, Blake and Pax had a baby on the way, and the others were enjoying newly wedded bliss. It was good for his team to be back on an even keel, and he was ready to move his own personal life to the next level.

He stood as Astrid walked through the door to the living room, knowing he wouldn't have much time before the surprise was ruined so he needed to move fast.

"Hey, handsome." She came straight to him for a kiss, and instantly he was seduced, mind and body by the feel of her lips on his. His hands roamed over the tight black jeans she wore to cup the cheeks of her ass, and she moaned against him.

Jack pulled away, needing to put space between them or he'd lose himself and take her to the couch and forget everything but how she felt and tasted. "I have a surprise for you."

Her eyes lit up, and he loved how she was such a big kid about gifts. Christmas had been so much fun because he got to watch her get so much joy from both the gifts she'd received and those she gave. Her generosity was one more thing he loved about her and it more than made up for the mountain of shoeboxes stacked in his previously spare room.

"You do? What is it?"

He led her to the couch and made her sit down. "Wait here and close your eyes."

She did as he asked. "Is it kinky, Jack?"

He smothered a laugh as he lifted the gift gently in his arms. "No, nothing kinky but if you want that later I'm sure I can think of something." In fact, his mind was now distracted with all sorts of ways he could make her kinky fantasy come true.

Walking over, he knelt on one knee in front of his firefly. "Open your eyes."

Astrid blinked, and he watched the joy cross her face as she took in the tiny, sleeping, Pomeranian puppy that fit in his palm.

"Oh, Jack." She took the pup from his hands, not catching on to the extent of things yet. Her hand stroked over the soft fur before her fingers caught on the tags. Her eyes lifted to his as she lifted them to see the diamond ring attached to the collar.

"Astrid, I know I fought it at first, but once I gave up the fight, I realised that you were the most exquisite, beautiful person both inside and out. Your courage and strength are a thing to behold, and I love you more than I can ever express. I want to spend the rest of my life loving you and raising a family with you at my side. Will you marry me?"

Astrid grabbed his cheeks and pulled him close as tears poured down her face, and the puppy lay sleeping between them. "Yes, Jack, I'll marry you."

"Oh, thank God." He kissed her softly and held her against him, relief pouring through him that she'd said yes.

Astrid pulled away with a laugh when the puppy squeaked. "Were you worried I'd say no?"

"Not really, but I wanted it to be special, and you never know for sure. You might have changed your mind." He took the ring from the pup's collar and pushed it onto her finger as she admired it. It was a beautiful solitaire diamond in a princess cut with a diamond band he knew would look gorgeous on her.

Jack got on the couch and pulled her across him so he could hold her close, settling the newest edition to their family on her lap.

"Never, Jack. You're never getting rid of me. Not ever."

"Good because I don't know what I would do without you in my life every day."

"Who would've thought when we met, we'd end up here."

"Not me. I thought you were a sexy pain in my ass determined to drive me crazy."

Her laughter rang through the house they shared and were making into a home where he hoped one day to raise their kids. "I thought you were sex on legs but also a stuck-up asshole who wouldn't know a good time if it bit him on the ass."

His fingers trailed over her shoulder, and she shivered at his touch, always so responsive to him. "Is that so?"

"Yep."

"I think that's a challenge."

"Not really. I learned long ago that you're not what I thought but if you want to see it that way, then there's only one winner here, and that's me."

His lips feathered over her neck. "Hmm, devious too. How about we put this guy to bed and take this celebration upstairs?"

"Cupid. His name is Cupid."

"Do you have any idea the shit I'll get for that?"

She turned and kissed him quick. "You're man enough to handle it."

He didn't know how she did it, but with no effort she made him feel like he could slay dragons and he still had some to slay for her, but they would wait. Tonight was about the future, not the past.

"Let's put him in his bed."

"Lead the way."

He led her to bed, where he had champagne and chocolate strawberries waiting for later, but for now, he just wanted to make love to the woman who would be his wife, his forever.

Later as they lay in bed, their limbs entwined so he didn't know where he finished and she began, he reflected on everything that had happened the last few years and knew despite everything, he wouldn't change a thing if it brought him here.

Astrid's head on his chest tipped up, so she was looking at him, her green, amber eyes soft and slumberous. "What are you thinking about?"

His fingers brushed her shoulder in slow sweeps. "Just how happy I am, and that I wouldn't change a thing."

She snuggled closer. "Me neither. This right here is the happiest

I've ever been, and each day keeps getting better. I know we'll face trials, but I also know we'll get through them."

"Those trials involve kids?" They had skirted the issue, but he was curious about what her thoughts were on starting a family.

"Kids are a blessing not a trial, Jack, and yes, I want four."

"Four!" He rolled until he'd pinned her to the bed with his body, his erection pressed against the heat of her.

Astrid wriggled against him, and he could feel the wetness of her desire against him. "Yes, four. Two boys and two girls."

"That's a lot."

"I know, but you'll be such an amazing dad."

"You think so?" He wanted kids but was determined not to repeat the mistakes his father had made.

"I know so."

Jack pressed his cock into her warm, tight pussy, and she whimpered a breathy sound as she clutched his shoulders, her eyes on him full of love he was never sure he'd be worthy of.

"Best get started then."

Her legs came around his waist, her feet resting on his ass as he moved inside her slowly. "Not until we're married and that can't happen until my sister can be beside me."

His lips found hers, and he slanted his mouth over hers, his tongue finding hers as he brought them both to climax, his seed spilling into her as she cried his name.

Jack held her tight to him when they were both spent. "I'll wait as long as you need, firefly, and I'll find the men who hurt her, and you, and make them pay."

"I know you will, and I know in my heart she'll find her way back to me."

Falling asleep that night in each other's arms, Jack knew he was the luckiest man alive because no matter what happened in his life, he had the woman he loved more than life beside him and a future that was beyond beautiful.

SNEAK PEEK: LOPEZ

He sat by her bed, his laptop open, working to find the answers he needed to solve this mystery. Adeline Lasson was a part of his past nobody knew about. Not even Jack or Will knew of the connection they shared, but he did. From the second he'd heard her name fall from Astrid's lips, the pieces had come together, falling into place.

Yet, before he could get the answers he so desperately needed, she was beaten, her voice silenced, and the answers he sought stolen once again. Lopez pushed his hair from his face, exhaustion once again plaguing him, but sleep was a rare thing for him. His mind was unable to relax and let go of the questions until his body took the choice from him and he collapsed into a deep sleep for twelve to fifteen hours, often waking feeling groggy and confused.

Jack understood his limits and knew of his past. He'd made no secret of who he was and what his past was or his desire to escape it, but nobody knew of the tether that kept him by the bed of the one woman who he hoped held the answers.

He should tell Jack the truth, tell Astrid, but after everything they'd been through, he had no desire to be the one to add more complications. There'd be time for that when Adeline woke—if she woke.

He'd been by her bedside for months. So much so, he knew her condition better than anyone, and there was no reason for her coma, at least not a physical one. Her body had healed, and her brain showed no irregularities from her injury, but that was where the complexities of the human body and mind came into play. The injuries she'd suffered were predictably unpredictable.

They'd never met or spoken in person, and yet he felt like he knew her, and he'd had the overwhelming desire to protect her and keep her safe from the people who hunted her. Looking back at his computer, he knew it would be quicker to go to Will and ask him to find the information, but he also knew once that pandora's box was opened, it couldn't be put back, and Adeline would be in danger once more.

Her finger twitched, and he placed the computer beside him and took her fingers in his. He noticed she got agitated easily and if he held her hand and spoke to her, she eased. "It's okay, Addie. Nobody is going to hurt you. You're safe, and I won't let anyone harm you ever again."

Instead of easing, her heart rate became more erratic, and she began to thrash around the bed until he had to stand, afraid she'd hurt herself. He hit the bell for the nurse who came running in to see what was wrong.

"I'll find the doctor."

Not knowing what else to do, Lopez sat on the bed and wrapped her lightly in his arms to stop her from hitting herself against the bars on the bed. As he looked down at her, a sob escaped her, cracking his heart in two at the pain inside it. Her eyes flew open, and he saw the bright green orbs for the first time. Fear clouded her face as she grasped at his arms, desperately weak but still fighting.

"Addie, it's okay. I'm a friend of Astrid's. You call her Bumble, right? And she calls you Bee."

Recognition cleared the fear, and she relaxed into him for a second, the weight of her feeling right in a way he didn't understand.

Her eyes moved back to his, and he waited for her to speak. "You have to help me, please." Her fingers clawed at him as she tried to sit up.

"What do you need?"

"My daughter. He has my daughter."

Then as if the effort that took was too much, she went slack in his arms, passed out cold, and Lopez felt a cold fear crawl up his spine. She had a child, and that child was missing, taken by someone. Even if it killed him, he'd get her back. Anything to take that look of desolation from her stunning face.

Order Lopez Now

BOOKS BY MADDIE WADE

Liam

Mitch

Gunner

Waggs

Jack

Lopez

———

Alliance Agency Series (co-written with India Kells)

Deadly Alliance

Knight Watch

Hidden Obsession

Lethal Justice

Innocent Target

———

Ryoshi Delta (part of Susan Stoker's Police and Fire: Operation Alpha World)

Condor's Vow

Sandstorm's Promise

Hawk's Honor

Omega's Oath

———

Tightrope Duet

Tightrope One

Tightrope Two

Angels of the Triad

01 Sariel

Other Worlds

Keeping Her Secrets *Suspenseful Seduction World* (Samantha A. Cole's World)

Finding English P*olice and Fire: Operation Alpha* (Susan Stoker's world)

ABOUT THE AUTHOR

Contact Me

If stalking an author is your thing and I sure hope it is then here are the links to my social media pages.

If you prefer your stalking to be more intimate, then my group Maddie's Minxes will welcome you with open arms.

General Email: info.maddiewade@gmail.com
Email: maddie@maddiewadeauthor.co.uk
Website: http://www.maddiewadeauthor.co.uk
Facebook page: https://www.facebook.com/maddieuk/
Facebook group: https://www.facebook.com/groups/546325035557882/
Amazon Author page: amazon.com/author/maddiewade
Goodreads: https://www.goodreads.com/author/show/14854265.Maddie_Wade
Bookbub: https://partners.bookbub.com/authors/3711690/edit
Twitter: @mwadeauthor
Pinterest: @maddie_wade
Instagram: Maddie Author

Printed in Great Britain
by Amazon